RED CREEK

A HORROR NOVEL
BY
NATHAN HYSTAD

This is a work of fiction. All of the characters, names, incidents, organizations, and dialogue in this novel are either products of the author's imagination or are used fictitiously.

The town of Red Creek in this book is in no way related to the real town of Red Creek, New York.

Cover art: Tom Edwards Design

Edited by: Scarlett R Algee

Formatted by: BZ Hercules

ISBN-13: 978-1719144612

ISBN-10: 1719144613

Also By Nathan Hystad

The Survivors Series

The Event

New Threat

New World

The Ancients

The Theos

One

*L*eaves rustled lightly around the park, reminding Paul that autumn was right around the corner. It was exceptionally warm for mid-September, and as usual, he was overdressed for the heat. He needed to find a better place to write, one with air conditioning. Sitting with a laptop propped on his knees, typing away while tourists gawked at the famous Central Park monuments, was how he'd written his first bestseller. Now it annoyed him and seemed to be nothing more than a constant reminder of his failures.

Paul looked at his word count and had the urge to toss the damned laptop into the lake, maybe even hitting a pair of lovebirds paddling by in their rented canoes. If only he could capture some of that magic again. No matter what he tried to duplicate about his first novel writing experience, he always fell flat. As much as he wanted to blame the setting, he knew better. It was him.

Back then, he'd been a wide-eyed newbie to the big city, starving for something that was far from success and bestseller lists. He'd written *The Underneath* with so much raw skill and passion, and the fifteen-years-later version of himself was lacking both of those things.

He stared at his blank screen, *Chapter Three* flashing on

the top of his document, two lonely words floating on a sea of white. Closing his eyes, he took four deep breaths, visualizing progress like his motivational podcasts told him to do. When he opened them, he still had nothing. He never did.

"Excuse me? Would you mind taking our picture?" a soft young voice asked. He thought about pretending he hadn't heard them, or maybe assuming they'd been speaking to someone else. In the end, he glanced up, happy to not be staring at his screen for a moment.

The girl couldn't have been over twenty and had a look only someone without hard years could pull off. Beside her stood a handsome young man, wearing pink shorts and a striped polo shirt. No doubt visiting the city from some rich suburb of Connecticut.

"Sure," was all Paul replied, taking her cell phone.

They moved into position in front of the water, the beautiful skyline of Manhattan covering the horizon. He played with the settings for a second, always sure to make the best of the first picture so he didn't have to keep taking them until one looked good.

The boy's arm wriggled around her slender waist, and he pulled her close. Paul thought she looked a little uncomfortable, but the girl quickly washed it away with a wide smile. It was hard to believe he'd ever been that young, innocent, and free of life's inevitable overwhelming weight.

"Cheese," he said, clicking a couple of shots and looking at the image. Something was beside them in the second one, something strange. He swiped back to it, and it was gone. He could have sworn there was a black shadowy figure behind the girl, but when he zoomed in, everything looked normal.

"Can we see?" the girl asked impatiently. He realized he must have seemed like a creep scrolling through her photos.

"Sorry, thought there was something on the lens. Here you go." Paul passed it back, happy to be done with the interaction. Since when had he become so annoyed with people? He used to be such a happy-go-lucky guy. It was something else on the ever-growing self-improvement list he had to work on.

The image of that familiar blurry shadow on the camera set something off in him. Ideas flooded his mind, and he saw the couple continue down the path, no doubt off to the fountain to find someone else to take their picture again. He had his muse. They usually came in the dark as he walked around moonlit streets. This one came in the middle of the hot afternoon, with only the cloud-shadows rolling over the park's expanse of green.

He'd gotten the spark for *The Underneath* at college. He and his friends had been drinking at the local watering hole, him looking old enough to sneak in at nineteen. He remembered having a test in the morning, so he'd left early, leaving them behind to hit on whatever was left at one AM. He'd walked the dark alleys, cutting his way to the dorms, when he'd seen it. A shadow moving of its own volition. It was always there in his periphery, but when he'd looked straight where it should be, it was gone. It had terrified him so much that he ran all the way back to his room, but the feeling of dread didn't leave him for a week. He couldn't tell anyone about it, because he knew no one would believe him. Plus, what was he going to say? A shadow scared him?

A couple weeks later, he finally accepted that he'd been drunk, and he'd always had an overactive imagination. But there was a spark from that experience, one that couldn't be tamed. He held on to that spark for a couple years and, it turned out, it just needed some kindling, which he found in New York when he moved there after college.

He felt the same spark course through him, and he highlighted his current work in progress. It was crap. He hit delete without a hint of regret at the loss of ten thousand words of rough-draft garbage. That wasn't the story he needed to tell. He had that now.

With a smile, he started to type.

***

"*W*e can get one point five for it," Don said through the speakerphone that sat on Paul's desk in his office.

"Are you kidding me? It's worth at least one point seven. You told me that yourself last year," Paul almost yelled.

"That was last year, and things change. This is New York City, and there are way more comparables going for quick sales right now. I'm sorry, but that's what I think you should ask for it. Of course, it's up to you in the end," Don said.

His friend was the professional. Some part of Paul was second-guessing selling the place, but without his wife and daughter around, he didn't need that much space. Terri had been asking him to sell it for a long time, even before they'd separated.

"Fine. How about you swing by tomorrow and we can go over the details?" Paul asked.

"Sounds like a plan. I'll bring dinner, you supply the wine. I assume you still have some of the stuff I like?" he asked.

"You bet. I saved a bottle for you," Paul lied. It was his wife's favorite too, and he'd always hoped to open it with her when they patched things up.

"How's the book going?"

Paul looked at this computer screen, seeing the pages

of words filled in the last few days. "It's going okay. I'll tell you about it when I see you." He felt like talking about it would jinx what he had going, and he hadn't had a rush of writing like this since that first book. The magic was back, and he was very superstitious about it.

The call ended with friendly goodbyes, and Paul leaned back in his leather chair. He was really going to miss this office. He spun slowly around in the chair, seeing his own novels lining the top shelf of his mahogany bookshelf, *The Underneath*'s movie poster framed above his gliding reading chair. The movie had been a bomb, but it was still based on his book, and that meant a lot to him. The poster showed a man standing in an alley, facing the camera, and shadows looming toward him, unseen. The tagline: *Just when you think things are on their way up, you find something dark buried underneath.*

He'd never quite loved the line and thought it was terribly cheesy, but they had gotten Freddie Prinze Jr. for the role of the main character, so that had been something. Of course, it was about ten years after his prime, so he hadn't quite been the draw he once might have been.

Clippings of *New York Times* bestseller lists in matching frames adorned the wall behind his desk. Terri had surprised him with those, but for the past two years, there wasn't a week that went by where he hadn't wanted to rip everything off his walls and toss them in the garbage. His old successes only seemed to feed his depression. Terri had told him he needed to stop focusing on the past, but some days, it was all he felt like he had to grab on to. What future was he going to have without her and Taylor?

He made his way back to his computer, shaking off his trip down memory lane. Terri was right sometimes; hell, she was right most of the time. He did need to get his mind out of that place. If he could have done that, maybe she wouldn't have left and taken the best thing he'd ever done in his life. Taylor smiled at him from her fourth-grade school picture, sitting on the left corner of his desk. A school he had never seen; a school across the country.

He went back to the computer, but after thinking about Taylor, he had the urge to call her. Looking at his clock, he saw it was almost midnight, and his daughter would be long asleep, even on the west coast. Terri had the right to move her life, but did she have to choose the damned opposite coast?

Letting the anger go, he took a deep breath, and with forced focus, he got back to his book. Soon he was typing away, letting the story carry him on a wave of words.

He awoke in the gliding chair, his Kindle in sleep mode in his lap. Rubbing his neck, he saw the start of the day's light sneak through his blinds and knew it was morning. Crossing the office, he pulled the window covering's string, giving him the view he'd paid almost a million dollars for ten years ago. Central Park filled the window, looking resplendent as the sun's rays began to hit it from the east. For the first time in over a year, Paul felt the urge to go for a morning run. He'd been putting off working out, except for walking, for a long time, and knew it would help his mental state. Now that he was working on something he was happy about, maybe it was time to get his body back in shape.

Before he could talk himself out of it, he stretched out his back, stiff from sleeping in a chair, and changed into shorts and a t-shirt, then laced up his brand-new pair of running shoes. He saw himself in his front hallway mirror, seeing a man about ten pounds overweight, but amazingly still in half-decent shape. Gray hair covered more of the sides of his head than brown now, but he could live with that. He wasn't the type of man to consider dyeing his hair.

He was getting older.

Slipping his key into the small zip pocket in his shorts, he made his way down to the elevator.

"Good morning, Mr. Alenn," Jim the doorman said. "Going out for a run?"

Paul was sure Jim would be surprised. He always seemed to be on duty when Paul made his way back from his late nights after sulking over a bottle of scotch on Columbus.

"You bet," Paul said.

"Enjoy the morning. It's a beautiful day out there."

The air was fresh, slightly cooler than he'd expected after the recent heat wave, but he reveled in it, feeling energy he hadn't had in a long time. Since well before Terri had left. Central Park West was quiet this early in the morning; the museum traffic and small food trucks wouldn't be picking up for a couple hours yet.

He did a fast-paced walk to start, already feeling his unused muscles beginning to warm up. By the time he entered the paths into Central Park, he'd sped up to a light jog, trying to control his breathing. The air reminded him that winter was coming, and he was looking forward to it. The muggy city heat was something he'd never gotten used to. Being from far upstate New York, where it could get warm but still have harsh winters, he'd seen all the seasons had to offer.

His body remembered the long runs his wife and he used to go on over the years. It was the only way he liked to exercise before a sedentary day of writing. When he saw Belvedere Castle, he pumped his legs harder, going into a nice paced run.

There were dozens of runners out—a variety of housewives, business men, and retirees—all enjoying the morning. Paul thought of his book as he made his way toward the east end of the park, his blood pushing hard at that point. It had been going so well, he hoped he could get the majority of the first draft done before he had to move out. He hadn't let himself think too far in the future, but maybe he would move out west as well. Be closer to Taylor... and Terri. She might put up a fight, but he was confident he could get her to come around, especially when she saw how well he was doing.

He approached one of the tunnels, and he tried to re-member its name from the audio tour he'd taken there so many years ago. Graywacke, he thought. The sun was now almost above most of the tall buildings from the Upper East Side, casting their shadows long, leaning toward him. Squinting, he saw something inside the tunnel, hugging the left side of the wall. In his books, he'd often used settings like that to hide ominous villains or monsters, or to create tension in the character's mind. He felt a meta moment as he ran.

When he looked again, nothing was there, so he kept on moving. Probably just a sun spot from looking into the light. It had been so long since he'd run that he hadn't even thought to bring his sunglasses. Even though he knew there was nothing to be afraid of, his blood ran cold as he passed under the fifty-foot-deep passageway. His speed picked up inside, and when he emerged into the daylight on the other side, he slowed down, taking the time to look back. In his periphery, he thought he could see a dark blurry object. He stopped and turned around, only to see an empty underpass.

He nervously chuckled to himself, deciding he'd better not go much further. It was time to go home, shower, eat, and get started on the day's writing. With a last glance to the tunnel, he headed back another way, determined to for-get his childish imagination.

Two

*H*is sister's face appeared on the desk monitor. She was usually quite put together, but right now, she looked exhausted.

"Hi, Beth. How're you doing?" he asked, feeling awkward as usual at his conversations with his sister.

"I'm okay, Paul. It's been a long week here," she said. *Here* was back home at Red Creek, where they'd grown up. He could see yellow leaves behind her through the kitchen window. Autumn always came earlier upstate than in the city. "How about you? You look good."

"Thanks. I've been trying to take better care of myself. I figure just because I don't have anyone at home nagging me to eat well, that I should still be an aware human. How's Mom?" he asked, waiting for a barrage of guilt-ridden comments about how bad of a son he was.

Beth slunk down in the screen, visibly deflating before his eyes. It reminded Paul of a full balloon being let go of, flying away in the breeze. "She's not good. We have to move her to Greenbriar this weekend."

He couldn't imagine his badger of a mother allowing anyone to take her out of that house. "Are you sure? She's okay with this?"

"Paul, you have no idea what it's been like. The dementia is getting worse, and she fell down the stairs yesterday. She ended up with only a sprained ankle, thank God, but we can't risk it again. I thought about having her move in here, but Darrel won't have any of it. Not that I blame him. She's a handful, and they know how to deal with people in her condition," Beth said.

"Her condition? I know you told me she was forgetful and stuff, but dementia?" Paul asked, his voice rising slightly.

"Maybe if you called her once in a while, or God forbid, visited us up here. While you're living in your upscale townhouse, we're down in the salt mines, trying to survive." The hurt in her voice was evident.

Paul felt ready to retaliate, but looking at his younger sister, the wind blew out of his sails. She was right about every little bit of it. "I'm sorry. What can I do?" he asked.

She looked visibly startled at his question, like it was beyond surprising he even bothered to ask. This pained him, and he added being supportive to his sister to his ever-growing list of self-improvements.

"I know you haven't been here in ages, and I hate asking you this, but can you come up this weekend? I'll move Mom Friday, but we're going to need to go through all her stuff. I can't afford to pay for Greenbriar, so we have to sell the house, and quick."

The idea of going to Red Creek hit a nerve so strongly, and he didn't know why. His childhood had been like that of any other kid growing up in a small town in America. He didn't look back at it with intensely great memories, but it had been okay. He'd had good friends and been safe. What more could he ask for? Yet there was this underlying dread of going back, and Paul couldn't quite put his finger on it. *Time to face your fears*, he thought. "I'll be there Saturday. Meet you at the house at one. I'll bring the coffee."

She smiled, and it looked like ten years lifted off her face. "Great. Thanks, Paul. That was exactly what I needed to hear." He could hear a kid calling out to her mom in the background and knew it must be Isabelle. She was seven now.

"Sounds good. Love you, sis." With that, the call ended, and Paul somehow felt good about his decision. It went against his gut, but what good had his gut ever gotten him, at least in the past ten or so years? No good at all.

As the screen went to his desktop image, the doorbell rang. He'd lost track of time on chapter eleven of his book. The protagonist, Clay, was about to head home from college for Thanksgiving, and his girlfriend had sounded strange on the phone. Not what he needed to worry about after being stalked the weekend before by a madman, claiming he knew what monster was buried in Clay's head.

Paul walked down the hall, passing the massive master bedroom that felt empty these days. His clothing took up a quarter of the walk-in closet, and his sparse bathroom supplies made the seven-foot vanity look pathetically oversized.

The hall led into his open-concept kitchen, dining, and living room, windows lining the space. It was mostly dark out, the sun setting earlier every night. Everything was sleek and modern, which was to his taste. Terri had wanted a more rustic feel, but he'd won that battle. In those days, he'd won most of them, but that had run out, and he found himself wishing he'd given in to her more often.

The bell rang again, and Paul hurried to the door. With a quick unlock and turn of the handle, he was face to face with his realtor and good friend, Don Bronstein. The man had impeccable taste and dressed like the high-end home seller he was. Paul was a confident man, not overly concerned with what people thought of him, but being beside Don always made him feel a little inadequate. Don also stood three inches taller than him, and that didn't help much.

"Paul! So good to see you," Don said, going in for a hug while Paul stuck out his hand for a shake. They ended up with a manly half-hug, half back-clap scenario.

"Good to see you too, buddy," Paul said, waving him in. Don carried a to-go bag from their favorite Thai place in Brooklyn. It smelled amazing.

"All the way from Williamsburg to your door. We might need to heat it up," he said, setting the food down on the kitchen island. They pulled out stools, and Paul popped the cork on the bottle of vintage wine Don had mentioned on the phone.

The pad Thai turned out to be just warm enough, and it tasted as amazing as always, especially with the full-bodied red to finish it off with.

"Well, that was about as good as it gets. How's Maria doing?" Paul asked, pouring another glass of wine.

Don shrugged and smiled. "We broke up a month ago."

"Let me guess, there's a new one already?" Paul asked, half-kidding.

"There might be. And her name might be Karen, and she might be working for me."

"Oh, that's going to end well. I can see it now." Paul sipped his wine, suddenly not wanting to sell. Sitting there with someone else in the house, actually having a meal in the kitchen? It felt like it had been so long, he'd almost forgotten what it was like. The place was still way too big for him.

"It always does. So you're sure about selling? It is beautiful. I think I may have underestimated the value. I forgot how sexy this renovation was." Don leaned back, swirling the wine in his glass.

"I think so. Hey, I'm heading up to Red Creek this

weekend. We need to sell my mother's house." Paul started to clean up the food, scraping the leftover pad Thai into a Tupperware.

"Red Creek? When's the last time you were up there?" Don asked.

"Twenty years. I haven't been back since I left. My mom's going to a home… or one of those assisted-living places." Paul was nervous to see his mom again, especially in her new condition. "Any chance you know someone up-state that could help?"

Don gave him a big realtor smile, hiding the fact that twenty years was basically forever. "Let me see what I can do. If I have to go there and sell it myself, it's the least I can do for one of my best friends in the world. Send me the address later and I'll check into it."

Paul was happy to hear that and knew he'd take his friend up on the offer if needed.

"How's the book going?"

Paul was hesitant to even talk about it, because it was going so well. "Great. I haven't felt this good about writing since *The Underneath*. Something clicked the other day, and it was as if all my barriers from the last twelve years disappeared. I was that free-spirited write-because-you-love-it kind of author again. I'd thought it was over." He'd honestly believed that for the past five years as he'd struggled to get publishers' interest, let alone get through a half-assed draft, even if they gave him the green light.

"That's great, Paul! That demands we have another drink. Don't worry, I took an Uber here, and we don't only have to drink the good stuff. By the bottom of this bottle, I'd probably drink something out of a box." Don was always a cheerful one, and Paul knew he should spend more time around the positive guy.

They talked about life, and what Paul's future might

hold now that his wife was out of the picture, with his daughter across the country. He didn't let Don know how much he wanted to have them back. He casually brushed off the idea of a double date but knew he'd eventually have to, since there was a bug in Don's ear about it now.

Before they knew it, it was one in the morning. Don looked like he was about to nod off, and Paul ushered him out the door, after using his phone app to get him a driver. Paul still hadn't gotten on with today's technology. He preferred the good old yellow taxis that zipped around the city like bees in a honeycomb.

The lights were dim in his living room. They were on the late-night setting he'd had installed with the automation package Terri had assured him was a total waste of money. Half drunk and full of food, it seemed like genius to him. Paul grabbed his laptop, sitting on the stiff leather chair. He'd complained to his wife about the lack of comfort when she'd had it delivered, but now he found himself gravitating toward it, like he deserved the punishment. Either that or he just missed her, and it reminded him she still existed.

Don needed his mom's house information, so he figured he might as well get that out of the way while it was fresh in his mind. It was a detail he was sure to forget come morning, when he planned on jogging again before getting back to the work in progress.

He opened the maps application, thinking it would be much easier to find the address on his computer than to search for it in the piles of useless papers he had stored somewhere in his office. When you were from a small town, you usually identified with landmarks, not a street address, so he didn't know it by heart. Come to think about it, he wasn't sure he'd ever even known his house number. Maybe he was getting old. His mother's dementia jumped to the forefront of his thoughts, and for the first time, Paul wondered if he would meet the same fate as her. He shrugged it off in his current state, assuming if anything, he'd die of a major heart attack like his father had.

"Good old trip down memory lane," he said aloud to no one.

He typed *Red Creek* into the search field and clicked the one in New York State. He hadn't ever looked to see if there were other towns with the same name. Another crappy small town with nothing to separate itself from anywhere else. Mediocrity at its finest.

An overhead drawing of the town appeared on the laptop, the few streets criss-crossing. He couldn't believe how small it looked. Population of three thousand. Had he really come from such a tiny place? Being in Manhattan every day, it seemed impossible to him.

He made out a landmark he knew well: the school near their house. It was one of those K-8 schools, mixing tiny kids with ones well on their way to thinking they were adults. From there, his mom's house was only a handful of blocks north, and he followed the line of homes backing onto farmland until he thought he was close.

He switched from line drawing to satellite image, and the yellow of the canola field shone up at him. He could see trampolines in yards and the pool down the street that no one was allowed to use. Old Mrs. Henderson's grandson had drowned in it one summer when Paul was little. They found him floating face down, fully clothed. Paul remembered watching them roll his small bloated body to the ambulance on a gurney. Even for a young boy, it was easy to tell the kid was dead. For the rest of his youth, the pool was shut down. Evidently, it still sat there, and full, by the looks of the reflection. He imagined old Mrs. Henderson had probably passed on by now. She'd seemed older than the pyramids back in the day, but a child's imagination could be extreme.

Then he saw his family house from above. The yard looked smaller than he remembered it, but images of him playing catch with his buddy Jason, or throwing water balloons at Beth and her friends, clouded his eyes. When was the last time he'd thought anything about that place? If you'd asked him any details a week ago, he was sure he would have drawn a blank. There was something about seeing it on screen that allowed things to flood back to him.

"Did Red Creek actually get the street view option?" he asked out loud again, feeling more comfortable in his empty place when he spoke to the air sometimes.

He dragged the little man icon onto the street and watched it zoom into a real image of the neighborhood. He landed at the neighbors', and he wondered if the Blaskies still lived there. A minivan was parked out front, and he guessed either one of their kids had taken it over, or they'd sold it to a young family. Things changed, even in small towns, at a slower pace.

His wine glass beckoned him and he sipped it, wishing he had opened a good bottle on the second go around.

"A man creeping on his old house on the internet at two AM shouldn't be a snob about what wine he's drinking by the gallon," Paul said to himself.

Moving down the street, he shifted the view to look directly at his mom's house. There were no cars in the driveway or on the street. The lawn looked too long, and the spruce tree that had been over eight feet tall when he'd left home was now thirty or so feet in the air. Guilt that his mother didn't have someone to help her with that stuff racked him, and he vowed to start helping more. He'd been so self-obsessed that he'd driven his family away, then his wife.

The house needed some paint and a little landscaping, but he was sure he could hire some kids to help out and increase the value. With determination, he took another drink and continued to move down the street on the 3D map. Memories of riding his bike and of different friends over the years hit him hard, and he took a moment to gather himself in his wine-fogged state of mind.

The street ended in a field, a bare patch of grass between the crops. It was always worn from all the kids walking out to the forested area, where they'd play army or try to build a tree fort.

He looked at the screen, seeing something in the distance. It looked blurry, but he was sure it was a person, with something black around them. A bike sat on the grassy entrance. He double-clicked, but the camera had stopped there, staying only on the streets. He could zoom in a bit, but the image was nothing but pixels.

Squinting, he could make out a small form, and it looked like he or she was floating in the air, lifted by the black smudge. His heart raced as he saw it, something clicking in his head, an old repressed memory of a hot summer twenty-five years ago. He couldn't make out why the fear was so strong, or what had happened, but the path he looked down on the screen narrowed, and all he could see was the blurry black spot and the trees in the distance. His wine splattered as the hand holding it shook suddenly, a spasm he'd never had before.

With a smack of the laptop, he closed it, getting up and walking away, feeling the urge to scream.

"It's nothing, you big baby," he said in a quivering voice. "You always get shaken up when writing a good book. That's all. Nothing happened back then, and it was probably a kid walking his dog in the picture."

It was four in the morning when Paul rolled over in his

king-sized bed and looked at the alarm clock. He closed his eyes, smelling musty crops and the scent of fall leaves on the ground.

Three

*P*aul rolled his suitcase across the hardwood floors, wondering if he'd over-packed for a weekend. That was a common occurrence for him when traveling. He'd bring four pairs of pants and end up wearing the jeans he drove in ninety percent of the time. He tried to be practical for heading back home, but there was a nagging worry that he couldn't be too overdressed, as if wearing a sport coat to dinner would rub it in the small townsfolk's faces that he was someone special to be seen. Then there'd be the polar opposite reaction if he didn't dress well enough; they'd think him a failure, tucking his tail between his legs and heading back home.

He suddenly wondered why he cared at all what the people of Red Creek thought about him. They hadn't meant anything to him when he'd lived there, and he certainly didn't stay awake at night wondering what had happened to any of them. Come to think of it, before talking to his sister, he'd almost completely forgotten about the town over the last year. He noted the human mind was always sure to worry about inconsequential things at the most inopportune times, and carried on, locking his door behind him.

The townhouse was clean and staged, ready for an

open house while he was away. Don had made it all happen so fast, and Paul couldn't help but feel a little rushed in the decision. That was wrong. The decision to sell had been overthought about for six months or so, but since finally pulling the trigger, it was like he'd blinked and the *For Sale* sign was up. He told himself it was a good thing, and his life was on the right track once again. The downward spiral he'd been in was over; he could now climb out of the primordial ooze he'd put himself into and experience a rebirth in his late thirties. It wasn't totally out of the question.

Jim smiled at him as he approached. "Going away for the weekend, Mr. Alenn?"

"Upstate. My old hometown," Paul said.

Jim looked a little surprised but kept his composure like any good doorman. They loved to gossip but didn't ever want to show the tenants. Paul knew he probably hadn't ever spoken about his past with the man, and even fewer fans knew about his hometown. It hadn't shown up on any of his book bios, and why would anyone care anyway? It wasn't like he was Stephen King.

"Excellent. I hope you enjoy yourself. Anything you need while you're away?" Jim asked.

"Now that you mention it, my friend Don Bronstein will be here later to make the final touches and pictures on my place, then he's holding an open house tomorrow." Paul realized he hadn't told the doorman yet, but Don claimed he was telling the condo board on his behalf.

"You're selling? That's disappointing. It's been a pleasure, Mr. Alenn," Jim said. Paul had always thought Jim nice enough.

"Likewise," Paul said, passing by Jim as he held the door open for him. His car was waiting out front, and he flipped the guy twenty bucks, checking for any out-of-place marks. His Beamer sat in the parking garage for weeks at a time, sometimes longer, without being driven. As he got into the driver's seat, he wondered when he'd last left the city. Sure, he'd driven to Jersey or Long Island a couple times, but actually on the interstate? Had to be the summer before.

The thought of heading back home hadn't seemed so bad, but as he fought traffic, alone in his own mind, he began to dread it. He hadn't seen Beth in so long. What a terrible uncle he was to the little girl that was a year younger than his own daughter. Terri used to send gifts, so he was sure he'd missed at least a Christmas and a birthday in the mix. Maybe he'd pick something up on the way. Beth's husband Darrel was all right, if a little cliché for Paul's liking. He'd grown up there, a couple years older than Paul. He remembered Darrel being a bit of a "townie," as he liked to think of them: plaid shirt, gun-toting, and beer-guzzling. But when you got around to it, he was friendlier than Paul had originally expected, and he took good care of Paul's little sister, which went a long way. At least someone was there for her.

His mother was another story. They'd never had a great relationship; she a bullish powerhouse, where Paul had been a soft boy. She'd walked over him, and when he'd finally stood up to her as he was about to go to college, she'd gone off on him and told him he wasn't welcome back. His dad had taken him aside, saying it would pass, and that she was upset that he was leaving. He was wrong.

Someone honked at him, a New Yorker's way of saying "I'm changing lanes." He slowed and honked back, continuing down the road. Soon he was out of the big city, heading north. It was almost noon when he gassed up, deciding to stop for a bite to eat. Who knew what was waiting for him at the house? Probably nothing but powdered milk and bacon fat.

The diner looked like the thousand others lining the roads of America, which was what he needed right then. He hadn't eaten anything that morning, still a little foggy from poor sleep that week. His car was parked on the gravel beside the gas station, the air outside a mix of gasoline and grease traps.

With his laptop in his hand, Paul figured he could fly through the end of the chapter he'd started the night before. It was on the tip of his brain, and it would ease onto the Word doc, no problem. Inside the diner was exactly as expected: a long bar lined with stools, booths along the sides, and tables covered in red and white tablecloths in the middle. Baseball jerseys and posters lined the side wall. It was classic Americana.

Taking a booth near the back, facing the door, Paul pulled out his computer and ordered a coffee, black.

Before opening his book file, the internet icon stared back at him. This place wouldn't have Wi-Fi anyway... would it? He clicked the little icon on the task bar and found Dot's Diner Free WIFI on there. With a press of a button, he was in. The path was overtaking most of his thoughts, the smell of leaves and canola bugging his olfactory sensors at the strangest times.

He started to type the address in, now that he knew it by heart. He'd gone to that street view image at least a dozen times since he'd found it the other night. Before he hit the enter key, the waitress came, giving him a steaming cup of joe, and asked him if he was ready to order.

"One more minute," he said, smiling, even though his back was dripping sweat and he was suddenly paralyzed with fear. She left, whistling some old song from the sixties, and he slammed the laptop shut. He was becoming obsessed with some memory that probably never happened. It was only stress about going back to Red Creek.

Feeling better about it, he scanned the laminated menu, settling on a tuna melt and fries. He could hear Terri's voice telling him to get the side salad, no dressing.

"Excuse me," he called to the waitress, who hadn't bothered to write his order down in the half-dead diner. "Can you change the fries to a salad, dressing on the side, please?"

Terri would be proud of him.

***

*T*he landscape became familiar. White ash and black willows littered the roadsides, and crops were being harvested, kicking up dust, the musty dry smell reminding him of his childhood. If things were the same, he'd be passing a pig farm on his left in a half mile and would be well on his way to the town limits. *Blink and you'd miss it*, his father had always said, and now that Paul was back, he knew just how true those words were.

Old farm equipment rusted on the side of the road, where the signs told him to slow to thirty. Ahead was the aged wooden sign that looked like it hadn't been painted since it was made, well before Paul was born. *Red Creek: Our home, your home.* What a slogan. It sure didn't feel like home, yet there was something in the pit of his stomach, and Paul wasn't sure if it was outright panic or a longing for something that once was. A simpler time, where he could hop on his bike and meet his friends at the park for a game of four-boy baseball. Or sneaking off with Jason in the middle of the night, to spy on Chrissy's house when she had the girls over for a sleepover.

He would ask Beth what happened to Jason; hell, even Chrissy, for that matter. They'd dated for a few months when he was a senior, if you could call going to the movies the next town over a few times and never getting past second base dating. Still, she'd been a cute girl the whole time Paul had known her, and he hoped her life had gone down a happy path. For that to happen, she'd have to have moved away.

Slamming on his brakes, he nearly smacked his face into the steering wheel as a kid darted out into the road on his BMX. He didn't even turn back or look Paul's way! Paul honked, rolling down his window. "Wear a helmet!" he yelled after the kid. He took a breath, then pulled ahead, worrying he was blocking traffic. He wasn't in Manhattan anymore. There were no cars behind him. *Of course not. It's two o'clock on a weekend. Why would anyone be out?*

A sheriff's car was pulled to the side of the road, its driver eating something tinfoil-wrapped. Their eyes met and Paul nodded, getting nothing but a hard stare back from the old man behind the wheel. So, it was going to be like that?

***

*T*he shriek of tires brought Cliff out of his burger-induced daze. He saw the O'Brian kid scoot out of the way, and the driver of a new Beamer yell something at him. Who in God's name was that? Red Creek didn't have too many tourists, especially after the school bells rang for the first time. The orchards had done their bit for the year, dropping hearty apples around, barely keeping what stood for an economy on the up and up.

Cliff took another bite, staring at the man as he drove off, seemingly in a hurry to get somewhere. He'd have to keep an eye out for the guy. If there was one thing Cliff didn't like, it was surprises in his town. The clock blinked at him, 2:05, and he wondered if he'd remembered to take his blood pressure pills. Damn it. Ethel always counted them, making sure he took them, and making him feel the fool if he'd forgotten. He'd probably taken them. He usually did.

Cliff took one last bite of the burger, mustard dripping from the tinfoil onto his beige uniform pants. "Son of a bitch!" he cursed, reaching for a napkin. He'd have to toss all evidence of his lunch too. Another thing Ethel liked to search for.

Remembering the salad and apple she'd packed him, he grabbed the brown bag in the back seat, eyeballing the garbage can that was just out of reach from his window. He got out, feeling none of the guilt he once had at throwing his wife's prepared lunches away. Once the bag was safely sitting at the bottom of the green can, he turned to get back into his car, but the picture on the telephone pole stopped him.

That damned Benning was still at it, stapling pictures of his son on every wooden post in town. Cliff knew he was missing, and so did the whole town, as if putting up a picture of the kid a year later was going to help the fact that he was probably dead in the forest, dragged away by some animal or another. Still, if there was one thing that got to Cliff at his ripe old I-don't-give-a-rat's-ass age, it was the kids he'd never been able to find over the years. The only one they'd gotten back was because of Cliff, not the local force. That still itched his feet the wrong way.

The boy in the picture smiled in the black and white eight-by-ten, wearing a Yankees shirt, his hair in a mad disarray that only an eleven-year-old boy could make. That case was closed, at least for Cliff. A year was a long time... especially for a lost child, or an abduction. A year was forever.

His radio chimed in from the car. Gloria going on about an accident on the highway. He hated dealing with accidents and considered radioing back to tell her he was occupied, and to let the state deal with it. But with a stuffed belly and a head full of regrets, he sauntered over to the cruiser, flipped his cherries on, and made for the collision.

Four

*P*aul entered Main Street, a hyperbole if there ever was one. The sidewalks were run-down; the lines on the angle parking down the street were in desperate need of a paint job. Had the town ever been this lowbrow when he'd lived here? Surely they'd let it go. For the first time in his life, he contemplated what economic void this place filled, and it had to be farming. There were also a lot of apple orchards a way north of Red Creek, but he doubted that business was much of a stimulant. Looking around, he felt sad for them. This wasn't right. They were living their lives, and many of them wouldn't trade it for the world. His snooty Upper West Side townhouse aside, this was where he came from. A landscaper once told him that a tree's roots were as large in the ground as the tree was tall: as above, so below. He was rooted to Red Creek.

His cell phone rang, Beth's name coming up on the caller ID. Paul hit the answer button on the steering wheel. "Hey, sis."

"It's after two. You said you'd be here at one," she said, less angry than he'd expected. She probably hadn't thought he'd actually show up.

"Sorry. I'm on the way. Be there in ten. Wait, this is Red Creek. Make it five."

"Don't forget the coffee. I need it today," she said, a lightness behind her voice: relief that he was about to arrive and help her with an immeasurable task nobody ever wants to embark on alone.

"Where's a good place? You don't have a Starbucks yet, I'm guessing," Paul said.

"Go to Chuck's on Main," she conveniently said right as he drove past it.

With a two-seventy turn, he pulled into the otherwise vacant strip of parking spots. "Okay, but Chuck better make it fresh every twenty minutes. Anything else while I'm here? French fries? I know how much you like them… gravy-drenched."

Beth made a scoffing noise. "That was twenty-something years ago, bucko. I'm not that pudgy little kid anymore." And after a two-second pause, "Bring the fries. Extra gravy."

The phone went dead, and Paul snickered to himself, feeling better about his return home. At least he'd have his little sister by his side. He did miss her. They'd had a tumultuous relationship over the years, but he loved her.

Chuck's door jingled as it passed by the dainty bells strung up inside the place.

Inside, two men sat at the breakfast bar; another classic American diner. They turned and eyed him up and down before rotating back and drinking their coffees.

"Friendly bunch," Paul said under his breath.

An affable man walked up from the back, white apron smudged with what could only be ten years' worth of bacon grease. He looked about Paul's age, a paunch pushing out under his apron. Squinting, Paul put the pieces together. "Charlie?"

The man smiled wide. "That's my name! What can I do you for?" he asked, hands clasped together.

"It's me, Paul. Paul Alenn!" He never thought he'd be this excited to see someone he was only half-friends with when he was a kid, but here he was, heart pounding as he talked to Charlie, or Chuck, as he must be going by now.

"Well, I'll be a gorilla's cousin! It's you!" Charlie said, crossing from behind the other side of the counter and pushing Paul's extended hand away, embracing him like they were old lovers. "How the hell have you been?" He was now holding Paul at arm's length, appraising him.

"I've been–" Paul paused, not sure how to answer it. "I've been good. I see you're the proud owner of this fine establishment. Good on you."

"Thanks. Not quite the same as being a big-time author, but it pays the bills."

Charlie was still smiling and led Paul to the end of the bar, gesturing for him to sit. Moments later, he had a cup of coffee in front of him.

"Beth said it's the only place to get a coffee in town, and now I know why. It's great," Paul said, and witnessed his old friend turn fire-truck red in an instant. "Oh, speaking of which, I have to meet her at the old house, and I'm already late. Can I get a rain check?"

"It so happens that a couple of the guys and I are going to O'Sullivan's for a few cold ones tonight. Why don't you come out?" Charlie asked, eyes wide.

Paul's gut told him it was a bad idea. First night in town and going out to get drunk with the locals? But he was one of them, in a way, and he wouldn't mind seeing what happened to some of his old buddies.

"Sure, why the hell not. Tell me, is Jason still around?" he asked.

Charlie got quiet, and his posture changed. "Yeah, but he's not much for coming out these days. I suppose you never did hear. His little boy went missing last summer. They never found him."

Paul felt like he'd been kicked. Why hadn't Beth told

him about that? He'd have come back and helped any way he could have. But the reality was, he probably wouldn't have. More likely he'd have emailed him condolences or a "Best Wishes" e-card.

"That's terrible." Charlie handed him another coffee to go, and Paul ordered the fries and gravy for Beth.

As he walked past the two old men, who hadn't seemed to say a word the whole time he was there, he called back, "See you tonight." With that, he was minutes away from his old house.

Driving up his old street was surreal. It looked exactly like it had in his memories, if not twenty years older. The trees were all larger, the roads more run-down, but the street view on his computer had prepared him for that. Thinking about that computer image almost made him drive straight past his mom's house, to the corner where the path would lead him between the fields and into the woods beyond. What was back there? He'd searched his memory for days, as he'd lain awake in bed, for the answer to that question. Deep down, he knew he'd been back there countless times as a little kid. He and Jason used to ride their bikes down there… and then the memory stopped.

"Paul?" a voice called, carrying into his open driver's side window. He turned to it and saw Beth standing on the doorstep, concern etched over her face.

Paul was stopped in the middle of the street, facing the pathway down the block. When he looked at the clock, he saw he must have been sitting there staring at it for at least five minutes. Something wet dripped down his lip and he reached for a tissue, thinking that the fall leaves out there must be playing with his allergies. He wiped, and it came away blood red. Startled, he grabbed another one and jammed it inside his nostril.

Beth was now walking toward him; he took one last

look at the path before gunning the car and turning around in a fast screech, to come back and park in front of their old house. Beth shook her head at him: an admonishing look, but mixed with happiness at seeing her big old silly brother. This warmed him and almost let him forget the fact that he'd lost five minutes and suffered a nosebleed. *It wasn't lost. You were overwhelmed by your overactive imagination.* Nosebleeds happened to people all the time, especially when the air wasn't as humid as the big city's.

"Everything okay?" Beth asked as Paul got out of the car.

He looked her over and bent in to get a big hug. It started like hugging an acquaintance at the Christmas party and evolved to something else. Beth held him tightly, her warm face leaking tears onto his neck while they held each other like only long-lost family could. Words that didn't need to be spoken were passed back and forth soundlessly as they stood in each other's arms.

"Paul, I…" she started to say and stopped as they broke the hug. She noticed his nose tissue and raised an eyebrow. "A nosebleed? You still get those all the time?"

All the time? He couldn't recall ever having them. "I guess so, but it's been a long time since I had one of these. Must be the dry air."

Beth looked different. He'd seen her on their computer conversations, but that was mostly their heads. In person, it was like seeing someone from your past in a time warp, even though they'd visited in the city a couple years ago. She'd put on another ten pounds, and her hair needed a dye job, thick dark roots ending four inches out into dirty blond streaks. She was still a beautiful girl, though. He almost laughed when he thought she must be thinking the same things about him. He sucked in his gut as she appraised him back.

The yard looked better than it had in the picture. Beth or her husband had likely trimmed the trees, weeded, and cut the thick grass. The outside of the house was in desperate need of some sanding and painting. If there was enough value in fixing it up, maybe he could hire some locals to do the work for his mom or get his own hands dirty. The idea would have made Terri laugh, but something about being here made him feel like a different man.

"Strange to be back?" Beth asked, watching him sidelong as they approached the home.

"More than you know. Mom's not here?" He knew she wouldn't be, unless Beth wanted to spring them on each other, hoping for a happy reunion.

"She's over at Greenbriar. The few minutes she was lucid, she was royally pissed at me. Other than that, she seemed to like the place." Her casual conversation about their sick mom sent another wave of guilt into Paul's gut. She'd had to deal with it all: Dad dying, then their mom's slow disintegration.

"I'm sorry, Beth," Paul said, noting the bags under his sister's eyes.

They stood at the front door, Beth's back toward him. "I know, Paul. Maybe we can forge a new path, starting today," she said quietly and perhaps a little hopefully. It broke his heart. He reached forward and grabbed her hand, holding the coffees and the bag of Chuck's fries in the other one.

The door opened, and the smell of his childhood rushed into his nose, flashes of memories stirring in fragments in the corner of his mind. He almost dropped the bag and swore as one of the coffees leaked onto his arm.

Stepping inside was like walking into a dream machine. The air felt thick, and he wasn't sure if it was stuffy or just his reaction to it. The floor was lined with the same brown carpet that had always been there – dark enough to hide most stains, their mom had said, and the two of them had put it to the test more than once. The walls were in need of a good paint job, and when Paul saw into the living room, he nearly dropped. It was filled with boxes.

"Did you already pack all of this stuff?" he asked.

"What do you mean?" Beth took the coffee from his hand, finally, and set it down on a box, leaving a wet ring on the cardboard. "Oh, you mean this *stuff.* Mom has changed a lot since you saw her last. She started to pack all of our things from when we were kids, and it ended up in the basement. When Dad passed away, she couldn't bear to part with any of his possessions, so she boxed it and moved all of it out here. She figured no one but me came around, and that gave her free rein to do whatever she wanted."

They made their way beyond the boxes and into the small kitchen. The dining room was on the left, half-blocked by cabinets hanging down from the middle of the ceiling. Paul recalled how many times his father had claimed he was going to do an upgrade on the kitchen for them, but never got to it. There were a lot of things he'd promised over the years and had failed to deliver.

Paul remembered the summer when he was supposed to go to baseball camp. All his friends were going, and all Paul needed was the two hundred bucks to make it happen. A glorious month at a camp, staying in cabins with Jason and the rest of the crew, away from everything, just sleeping, eating, and playing their favorite sport, baseball. The week before he was supposed to leave, his dad told him he wasn't going. Something about the truck needing a new water pump, or some other lame excuse.

That summer ended up the worst of his young childhood. Paul nearly dropped his coffee as images flashed behind his eyelids. Hay on a dirt ground, a lantern swinging from a rope tied around a wooden beam. And the smells. A barn. Rotting leaves. Was that the sound of dripping water?

He could hear Beth's voice, small and tinny, as if she spoke to him through an old can and string. His eyes were open, but all he could see was the hay and the lantern.

"Paul!" Beth slapped him hard across the cheek and he came out of it as quickly as he'd disappeared.

"What the hell?" he asked loudly.

"You were spacing out! I didn't know what else to do," Beth said, voice panicked. Truthfully, he hadn't meant the question for her.

"I don't know what that was all about, but I'm thinking the whole 'coming back home' day has been a lot to take in. I've been heavy into this new book too, and it's darker than anything I've done before. I remember getting like this when I wrote *The Underneath*," he lied. He had been a little off when he'd written it, but nothing like what he'd just experienced, and not with a side of nosebleed.

"Well, you scared me half to death. I don't know how you can even write that stuff, to even think it up. I still can't believe I ever made it through that book. The movie was a little more bearable, at least," Beth said, and that was a sore spot for him. The movie took the easy way out when it came to the shadows, an interpretation he'd told the screenwriters was wrong over and over. They hadn't listened to him, saying it was too much for a wide audience. They'd probably been right, not that their version had made it into a blockbuster.

"It's called fiction. I'm a guy who likes to write horror. I *have* dabbled in some other genres, you know." This came out a little defiantly. His agent had almost laughed when Paul told him about the literary fiction book he'd started to write.

"Really? What kind of books?" she asked, sipping her coffee while sitting at the cluttered wooden kitchen table.

"I'd rather not get into it. I started it right after Terri left." The air seemed to leak out of his tires, and he sat at the table beside her, knees touching, and took a sip of his own coffee. It was surprisingly good, for Red Creek.

"How are they?"

"Terri has been effectively absent for the last year. Nothing but the cordial conversation for me. Taylor seems good. She recently started fifth grade. I can't believe it's been two years. Living alone in the empty townhouse, not writing anything worth my weight in garbage the whole time." Beth touched his arm, and he felt the urge to cry for the first time in a long time. If only his fans could see him now. She didn't say anything, just listened. "I kept thinking she'd come back, month after month, in complete denial of them leaving. California. Son of a bitch. Who uproots someone's kid to the other side of the country? May as well be in a different country. I've seen her three times. It's never a good time, she says, never convenient. She has no problem taking my money every month, so she can live on the beach and take surf lessons."

Paul took another drink of coffee and opened the fries, suddenly hungry even though he'd eaten the tuna only a couple hours before. It felt like days. "I think I realized they were gone for good. I was trying to write some piece of crap book in the park, and a couple came by asking me to take their picture. They were so young and in love. It felt like looking in a time machine, only she held his hand a little tighter than Terri had held mine, and he had a goofier look in his eyes than I ever had. It was there that everything changed." He skipped the part about the black spot in the picture that apparently only he'd seen. "I got an idea, a spark of a story at that moment. I'm thirty thousand words into it now, and I think it's the best thing I've ever written. Not that the bar's too high." Self-deprecation: an author's best line of defense.

"That's great. On both fronts. Acceptance is important to self-growth." It sounded to Paul like she'd read some of the same books on the subject as he had.

"And how about you? Things with Darrel okay?" He always hoped she was being taken care of and had wished nothing but the best for her. He wasn't sold that Darrel was the right choice, but who was he to judge?

Her posture changed, back straightening a bit. "He's... he's Darrel. Sometimes I think he's only in it because he started it. We hardly sleep in the same bed anymore. He blames his out-of-the-norm schedule and snoring, but when I suggest he gets a sleep test, he shrugs it off. Isabelle loves him so much, and he would do anything for her, but he only has room for one princess in his life, and it's not me."

Paul was taken a little aback that she was being so open with him, but it was utterly refreshing. In his normal life in New York, it was all about positioning and pomp. Everyone wore a veneer over their real selves, even his closest friends.

"I'm sorry, sis. That must be tough. I know what it's like when you have a kid and you cease to exist. Maybe we're destined to be unhappy. Look at Mom and Dad. It's in our genes." Paul had never really given his parents' relationship too much thought before, but he now knew they always seemed unhappy. Sure, most memories of one's childhood seem to focus on the good things— vacations, new bikes, first days of school—but rarely the scowls and days of non-conversation between parents. With his own family, things had always seemed tense around the house, and it got worse when he was a little older. Beth would have been around ten when the change happened.

"Do you ever remember Mom and Dad being happy?" Paul asked.

She smiled and nodded slowly. "I was six. You were off with your friends, playing in the park, or doing whatever you guys did. Probably chasing Chrissy around." She paused long enough to watch the color of Paul's face turn beet red. "Anyway... they took me up to Granny Smith's Orchard, you know, the big one off the highway north of town? We walked the orchard, me in between them, holding each of their hands.

"We tried different apples and had cider. Mom even bought a bottle of apple wine, though I don't remember them ever drinking it." She was looking out the window, as if seeking a simpler time, as many people did when they were so totally entrenched in adulthood that there was no turning back. "I remember seeing Mom and Dad holding hands there in the tree-lined fields, and at that time, I thought it was normal. The sad thing, even there on one of my favorite days as a little girl, looking back, I do feel like they were pretending to be happy there. For my benefit, and that makes it all the sadder." Her eyes were filling up with tears, a dam about to burst.

"What are you going to do about Darrel?" Paul asked, hoping to change the subject. Women crying around him was one of his top five most-dreaded things. It was one of the many faults Terri had listed off for him before she'd left.

A couple of the tears fell down her cheeks, quickly rubbed away as if she was ashamed of them. "I don't know. I just don't know."

"Beth, I know I've said this before, but I'm here for you now." He meant it. The change he felt within himself was real. He had the urge to get his laptop and start writing. Having his college kid return home was something he could really channel into at that moment. He assured himself the feeling wouldn't disappear before he got to work on it again.

"Thanks, Paul. I'm super glad you're here. The idea of doing all of this alone... it's too much."

"Speaking of which, where does a guy stay in a town like this? Is the old Red Creek Motel still up and running?" Paul asked, thinking about the rumors centered around the place over the years. Dead bodies under mattresses, cockroaches the size of your fist scurrying around while you slept, and best of all, the owner was a vampire. Paul bet two of the three were made up.

"Stay here, Paul," Beth said rolling her eyes at the sheer notion he'd consider sleeping in that pit of a motel. The idea hadn't crossed his mind, but now that he was there, sitting in the kitchen, it seemed like a good idea.

"I don't want to impose," he said.

"Who are you imposing on? Mom's staring off into the distance at Greenbriar. She kept your old room the same as it was." Beth was looking down, pecking at some of the fries.

He was a little taken aback. It had been almost twenty years; surely she wouldn't have left his stuff in the room that whole time? "What about all the boxes out here? Isn't my stuff in there?"

"Yeah. It's your old school stuff, your toys, worn-out clothes. I think she said there were even a couple stories from when you were a kid in there. I hadn't even known you dabbled back then," Beth said.

Had he? Paul didn't recall getting the writing bug until college, but it made sense. Most authors he'd met in the publishing circles all had the calling at a young age. Maybe he'd dig them out if he had time. Speaking of which… "So, what's the plan?"

She stared at him blankly for a moment, as if she was thinking about a deeper meaning behind his innocent question. "Beth, I mean for the house."

The bags under her eyes looked more pronounced suddenly. "We have to pack this place up, donate what we can, then throw away the rest. We should sell what we can too, if there's anything worth selling. Everything is so old."

Paul thought about one of Terri's closest friends, who was always out for an antique hunt of some kind.

"Sometimes old things are valuable things. Who knows what we'll find among this ramble of a house? With Mom, maybe a secret stash of dollar bills tucked behind the walls. I seem to recall her disdain for banks." Paul could picture her sitting there at the kitchen table, bills covering every inch, while their father hid in the living room, watching the news, sipping a sweating Coors. Her hair would be a mess of dark brown curls, gray seeping in. His parents hadn't met until they were in their mid-thirties, and she'd gotten pregnant with Paul when she was thirty-seven.

By the time she was fifty, Beth was ten and Paul almost thirteen, and their dad was out of work. She worked at the school as a librarian but working a six-hour day at the local school hardly paid the bills. That particular day, his dad had come home to a table full of bills, and after a quick yelling match during which the two kids thought it better to hide in the basement, he'd taken his beer, and she was left to navigate the arduous Alenn finances.

It had been the first time Paul knew they were poor. His dad did odd jobs, working as a farm hand, driving tractors when the big guys' harvest time came, and delivering apples for some of the orchards. While the other kids were getting new shoes with pumps on the tongues, he was stuck wearing the kind that never quite gripped that wooden gymnasium floor properly. For the most part, he'd been okay with it because even at that young age, he'd understood.

Beth was still sitting there, the task at hand too large to get started on. Paul decided to tentatively take the leadership role and to see how Beth reacted to it. If she pushed back, he was happy to relinquish the role, never saying a word about it. If she went along with it, he would plod on and get the house in order. It sounded like a good plan.

"How about we start right here in the kitchen? I see you have boxes and tissue paper. Terri would always use the linens to pack up glassware. That way, you're packing two sections at once. What do you say?" Paul asked, smiling wide.

"I say that sounds perfect." They got to work, boxing up the kitchen cabinets from left to right. They laughed about odd things, like who used which glass the most, and how hideous the white and brown Corningware was.

Before they knew it, the sun was down, and Beth was getting a call from home, Darrel wondering when dinner was. She rolled her eyes at this, telling Paul that her husband would starve if she left him tied in a kitchen with a fridge full of food. He wouldn't even know how to open the door, even with his opposable thumbs.

She invited Paul over, but in the end, he claimed he was too tired, and was meeting up with the guys later for a drink. He'd get wings there. Truthfully, he wanted to take baby steps in Red Creek. Diving head first by spending the evening with Darrel and Isabelle felt too forced to him. He promised her tomorrow night and felt she knew the truth when she looked at him with sad eyes, but she smiled and nodded softly.

Beth followed his lead when he said they would move

to the living room, and on to the bedrooms tomorrow. Seeing progress was great for them both, and the daunting task was becoming a little like a renewed bonding session for the siblings.

They parted ways, Paul's sister walking down the front sidewalk to her beat-up Jeep. She drove off the way he'd come, and he watched her as the dim yellow street lights cast their eerie glow down the road. Turning around, he stopped as the pathway a couple houses down seemed to whisper his name. His arms instantly covered in goose-bumps, but he told himself it was nothing more than the crisp fall evening. An urge to walk the few steps down the street, and to continue to the worn path between the crops into the forested area beyond, overtook him. He was already a house over when he snapped out of it. What was it about that path that had him so enthralled?

His over-imaginative mind, seeing it on that damned street view program, was to blame. He'd been half drunk, and the image leant itself to the shadows he'd seen so many years ago down that alley in college, the ones he'd written a bestseller about. Did he seek to search out something to give him inspiration again? The black shadow behind the girl in the Central Park picture had set his writing juices going, and he didn't feel like it was a well about to run dry, so why focus on this path?

Still, he did want to see what was down there these days. Maybe the tree fort he and Jason had built was still there, a half-assed platform in an oversized oak.

The urge dissipated, and Paul checked his watch; a quarter past seven. Chuck and the gang would be at O'Sullivan's by now, no doubt on their second or third pitcher of Coors. He checked his outfit as he went back inside and decided to change his shirt. It was covered in dust from packing all day. Rolling his suitcase down the hall, he opened his old bedroom door for the first time in twenty years. The stale smell of dusty linens hit him like a wave. When was the last time someone had been inside?

It was like he'd stepped back into his time machine and ended up in the nineties. Baseball posters covered the wall behind his desk, Yankees all the way. He smiled at the few trophies that lined the bookcases; such crowning achievements at the time, they now felt like participation trophies for a kid who was better at thinking up stories than catching a ball. His bookshelf had copious amounts of old science fiction and fantasy books, some classic thin pulp fiction, and others the massive series tomes of the never-ending epic fantasy he'd been so obsessed with.

He thumbed through a few of them, smelling the paper like he'd done since he was a kid. As much as he loved digital reading now, something about those old paperbacks made him feel warm and fuzzy inside. Sitting on the bed, he smiled, remembering lying there staring at the popcorn ceiling thinking about Chrissy, or about the days he could leave Red Creek and start his real life. Staring up at it again while smelling the stale bedsheets, he could only think of Terri and Taylor.

Before he let himself get dragged down into another bout of depressed thoughts, he grabbed a fresh shirt and some deodorant and left the house, locking the door on the way out. Not that anyone would break in. He hadn't seen a car drive by since he got here.

In a minute, he was heading back toward Main Street, his stomach in small knots at seeing his old friends after so long. The night was just beginning.

Five

"*I* said Central Park West!" Terri called to the cabby from the back seat. He seemed to be hard of hearing, or maybe the half-inch-thick plastic wall between them was muffling her words. He shrugged apologetically and stopped the meter early as he turned down a side street, finally heading in the right direction. It was dark down the Manhattan streets, and after being away for two years, it felt closed off, leaving her feeling a little claustrophobic and uneasy.

Taylor dozed on her shoulder as they stopped in front of their old home, its beautiful stonework evident even in the ominous late hour. Part of her missed that life, and another part wanted to tell the taxi driver to take them right back to JFK.

"Mom, are we home?" Taylor asked, little hands rubbing the sleep from her eyes. The words stung Terri as soon as they hit her ears. This wasn't their home, not anymore, but Taylor had been born here and lived the first six years of her life in the townhouse, so she smiled and nodded.

"We're at Daddy's," she said, suddenly wishing she hadn't surprised Paul with a pop by. It was more than a pop by, it was a "can we stay with you for a week or so," which she expected to last more than a week.

"Is Grandpa going to be okay?" Taylor asked for the

second or third time that day.

"I don't know, sweetie, but I sure hope so," she said quietly as they rolled their luggage toward the door. A tired-looking familiar face held the door open.

"Jim!" Terri said, embracing the middle-aged doorman.

He looked surprised but quickly merged his question-ing face into a wide smile. "Mrs. Alenn, it's so nice to see you. And Miss Alenn, you look so big!" Taylor gave the man a big hug around the waist, and he smiled even wider. Terri cringed when he called her by her married name, but he wouldn't have known she'd returned to her maiden name Henry, even though the divorce wasn't final yet.

"Relegated to the night shift, hey? Forget to water Ms. Kelley's ficus again?" Terri laughed.

He shifted uncomfortably. "No, we all take a few nights to make it easier on the new guys… and Ms. Kelley passed last year."

Terri felt horrible. Why hadn't Paul told her? Then she remembered she could count the phone calls over the last year on one of her hands, and only because she refused to answer his weekly calls to Taylor. "I'm sorry to hear that," she said, starting for the elevator.

"Where are you going?" Jim asked, jogging between them and her goal.

"We're going to *our* townhouse," she said, a little snip-pier than intended.

"It's for sale. Mr. Bronstein's showing it this weekend."

The words shocked her. Paul was finally selling the place. She'd been telling him to for years, and now he was doing it, which meant he'd given up on the hope of her and Taylor ever coming back. Terri felt relief, mixed with a little sadness.

"Well, my name's still on the deed, and I'm going up," she said, and pushed the up-arrow button. He stepped back, and when the doors opened, Jim was back behind his little desk along the wall.

"Goodnight, Jim," Taylor called, bringing a smile to the man once again.

The elevator doors closed, and she rested her head against the wooden sides of it while Taylor pressed the round *Three*. She'd remembered it, of course. The small space was almost too much as they took the short ride: the two of them, their luggage, along with the distinct odor of Mr. Martin's dog's urine. He never seemed fast enough to hobble down the hall and then outside, and the dog seemed to think hardwood was a good substitute for the Manhattan sidewalks.

A soft stop, and the doors opened, their suite at the far end of the hall. She spotted the bright red FOR SALE sign from back there, and the sight of it set her stomach flopping. Why should she care? She'd nagged him to do it, so why did she feel so bad about seeing it?

"Come on, honey, let's try to keep quiet. You know how noise carries down these halls," she whispered, checking her watch. It was after midnight, and their luggage wheels rolled louder than ever as they pulled them down the corridor.

Taylor was about to knock when Terri reached for her hand and patted it down. She jiggled her keys, hoping they would still work. Maybe they would frighten Paul by sneaking in, but somehow it felt like she was in control if she entered of her own volition. She didn't want him to *invite* her in, like some desperate ex-spouse in need of sanctuary.

"I should have gotten us a hotel," she said under her breath, just loud enough for Taylor to hear her. It was underhanded to get Taylor to always take her side, but it was part of the never-ending power struggle of the unhappily married.

The key slid in fine and turned smoothly, a light click rewarding her efforts. With a push, they were back in their old home.

The lights came on dimly as they entered, the occupancy sensors triggered. It looked so clean and tidy; then she remembered Jim had said they were showing it. Don must have had a fun time getting Paul to straighten up... or maybe two years alone had taught the man to do something around the house.

Forcing a gust of air out of pressed lips, Terri tried to let the anger and resentment go. If she was going to stay here, she would have to get over her petty nitpicks of her husband. He really could be a sweet man.

The smells of the home rushed her back to a memory of their first night there with Taylor. They sat together on the couch, Paul's new baby girl swaddled and drooling on his neck as she slept like a log. He'd been so great with her—changing diapers, helping to feed her—and kept being great with her until the day Terri had swiped her from his loving arms. God, she was a terrible jealous wench.

"Mommy, can I go see Daddy?" Taylor asked, eyes wide.

She nodded to her daughter, who ran through the kitchen and into the hall.

Shoes off, Terri's feet were spilling out their relief when Taylor came back, the look of a tantrum about to burst on her face. "Daddy's not here," she said, eyes welling with tears.

Terri passed through the place with quick efficiency, heading straight into their old room; Paul's room, now. It looked just as it had, and she felt like an invader. Her pillow was still in its spot, and the Himalayan salt lamp she'd left was still on her night stand. Paul had always talked to her like he longed for her back, without saying as much, and suddenly, she felt it in her soul. The man hadn't moved on at all. He'd spent two years there waiting for his wife and daughter, and she'd taken everything from him. If only she'd helped him, instead of pushing him away.

Her daughter's big eyes met her own, and Terri told herself that she'd done it for their little girl, because something dark lived in her husband, something that he hadn't been able to see. But she had, and at times it scared her to death.

"I'll call him in the morning, sweetie. Go to your room, and we'll make sure your bed is all made," Terri said, hugging Taylor close.

***

"You're telling me you never even thought about nailing that little blonde number from the movie?" Tyler asked, slurring every word like a man only could after eight or nine beers.

Paul shrugged it off. The night had started off kind of fun, getting to see his old buddies, but they didn't have a lot in common anymore. "Listen, I didn't sleep with anyone on the movie set, and I don't go to book signings to hook up with the hot stay-at-home moms who read my stuff. I'm married." He fidgeted with his wedding band, wondering all of a sudden if Terri still wore hers.

Charlie, or Chuck as he was now known, was at the bar getting them another round, which Paul knew was a horrible idea, but he didn't want to be the big wimp coming back to town and bitching out after only a few hours. Instead, he let the big truck drivers and construction guys pound back the beers, while he sipped his whiskey and walked the line between sober and splendid. A blonde woman slid up to Chuck while he was leaning over, paying for the pitchers. She gave Paul a look that could only mean one thing as Chuck blushed and said a few words, leaving the woman standing there, jeans so tight she'd need pliers to get them off.

"Who's that?" Paul asked, a frog appearing in his throat.

Tyler and Nick laughed, almost spilling their newfound beers as they shook the table.

"That's the ripest fruit for the picking in Red Creek," Nick said, smacking his lips. "She must only date out-of-towners, 'cause she keeps turning me down."

Paul tried to imagine that woman on a date with the bull of a man before him, in all his cut-off-sleeve glory. "I'm sure she has you misunderstood," he said instead. Nick nodded and took another drink.

Before Paul could find an excuse to leave, the bar doors opened and a man walked in, a cool breeze following him from the crisp fall night outside. The bar got noticeably quiet for a moment, almost as if the jukebox volume lowered, and the loud drunken Saturday night jabber went to whispers. The woman at the bar turned, taking her Corona and sauntering away, back to her friends.

The newcomer nodded softly to Chuck as he passed and took up a stool at the end of the bar, his back to the patrons. As soon as Paul saw him sitting from behind, he knew his old friend in an instant. He'd sat behind him in classes for years, and there was no mistaking Jason. "Why'd everyone get all weird when he came in?" he asked.

"Because Jason isn't the same man. He's angry. Best to stay away," Tyler said, the joviality gone from his voice.

Chuck became the voice of reason. "Jason isn't a bad guy. I know you guys were thick as thieves growing up, Paul, but he has a dark edge to him now. Can you imagine losing a kid like that?" Paul was finding himself liking the restaurant owner.

He smiled at Chuck. "I think I can handle the darkness. I'm going to talk to him." Ignoring his table's hushed comments about staying put, he crossed the bar, people watching him sidelong as he approached Jason. His old friend had on a blue Mets hat and a dirty denim jacket. He didn't move as Paul stood right beside him, close enough to touch elbows. Jason held a deep glass of brown liquid, whiskey probably. At least they had that in common.

"Bartender, I'll take another." Paul set a fiver on the bar top. In Manhattan, that wouldn't get him half a drink at a decent place.

Jason still hadn't turned to him, so Paul stood right where he was, looking forward. "I'm sorry to hear about your son," he said quietly, but loud enough for only Jason to hear him.

That got his attention, but not in the way Paul was hoping. Jason stood up so fast Paul was shoved backwards. He didn't say anything, but his fist went flying, smacking Paul beneath his left eye. Pain erupted, but Paul still stood, until the next blow hit him in the gut. Doubling over, he tried to grab his breath and put his arms up, but it was too late. Jason had kicked him in the side, and he crumpled to the bar's sticky floor.

"What the hell did you say?" Jason growled. He went to kick again, but Paul finally found his voice.

"Jay, it's me. Paul. Paul Alenn." The words floated out and Jason stopped, the look of rage melting away from his deeply lined face.

"Paul?" was all he said back.

Finally, a hand reached down, and Jason was looming over him. A second later, Paul was leaning on a stool, embarrassed that he'd gone down so easily. Jason always had been the tough one, and more than once, he'd stood up for Paul against bullies.

"What the hell are you doing here?" Jason asked, taking a long pull from his whiskey. Paul copied him, then wiped his mouth with his plaid sleeve. Surprisingly, no blood came back with it.

"My mom's not well; they moved her to Greenbriar. I'm helping Beth with the house."

"Look, I'm sorry about hitting you." Their eyes locked, and Paul stepped back. Jason's eyes looked black, darker than they had been as a kid.

Paul shrugged. "I've had a few tonight and didn't consider what you'd think of a stranger saying that to you." Jason waved the bartender down, and the tall young man didn't have to be asked twice. He brought fresh glasses and a bottle of Jack. Jason smiled tightly and thanked him. They moved over to a table at the far end of the bar, where the music was a little quieter and no one was lingering.

Paul waved to Chuck, letting him know everything was okay.

"I can't believe you're here. You look great. Well, except for that big red spot on your cheek." Jason smiled, genuinely this time, and Paul could see that youthful face from his childhood glimmering in there still.

"Thanks. I'm trying to get my shit together. I didn't know about your kid; otherwise, I'd have come back." Paul hoped the words sounded honest enough.

"Nothing you could do. He disappeared. Thin air. Vanished. Cops got nothing. They never even found his bike."

The blonde woman that had been eyeballing him earlier walked by with her jacket on, leaving a card behind on the sticky table. She didn't say a word, and neither did Paul. He nervously twisted his wedding band around his finger as she walked out the door.

"You know her?" Jason asked.

"Nope." Paul flipped the card between his fingers. "Apparently, she's Katherine Smith, and she's the marketing director for Granny Smith's Orchard. I smell nepotism. Wait, how do you not know her? I mean, it's not like this is a bustling urban community."

Jason shrugged, taking another drink. "Must be new. Maybe a cousin come to reap the rewards of the luxurious orchard life. Hey, aren't you married?"

"Yep. Well, separated. It's a long story." One he didn't want to get into with a guy he hadn't seen in twenty years.

"I hear that. Mary and I split too."

Paul didn't ask any questions. Losing a child was one of the worst possible things in life, and the strain would either bring a couple together or destroy them. No words were needed, instead they started talking about the old days, Paul enjoying rehashing the past.

Before he knew it, the lights were coming on, and the bottle was empty. Chuck and the others had left an hour or so before, and his drunken mind still felt guilty for ditching them. He'd hugged them and assured them all he'd have them over to the house in a couple of days. In the back of his mind, somewhere a sober brain cell regretted it as soon as he said it, but in his current state, all was well and happy.

"It was great catching up, Jay," Paul said as they stood in the parking lot. Jason headed for his truck, assuring Paul he lived only two minutes away. A lot could happen in two minutes. Paul opted to walk back, figuring the fresh air would do him good. He hadn't been whiskey-drunk in years, and it was starting to disagree with him.

The walk took longer than he thought it would, and by the time he made it to the right block after a couple of wrong turns, he was shivering. He ended up on the far side of the street, the pathway leading to the fields up to his right. The streetlights were out at the entrance, and he wanted to cross the street, away from the path, but his legs wouldn't let him. Something moved down the way, between the fields. In the darkness, it was nothing more than a shadow. Going against every bone in his body, Paul stepped onto the worn grass path with his left foot.

Six

Sheriff Cliff got in his squad car, his shirt untucked and wrinkled. Damn wife, couldn't even iron his clothes. He could still taste the sour rum in his mouth from last night's party, and wished he'd taken the time to brush his teeth. Gloria had called with such urgency, he'd thrown something on and left.

This time, it wasn't another highway fender bender. It was something strange, she said. The Hendersons had called it in.

Crossing town, he made his way to Wood Street, a neighborhood much like the rest in Red Creek: old and unkempt. At the end where fields lined the road between streets, he stopped, leaving the lights flashing but being nice enough to keep the siren off. Who was he kidding? That was for his own headache's benefit.

Otherwise, it was an idyllic autumn morning: light wind blowing the scent of newly fallen foliage, leaves rustling beneath his boots. He took a deep breath and almost forgot it was Sunday at seven AM. The pathway led between two fields of canola that had now been harvested. It went about half a mile before the treeline that led into someone's land. Most of the farms or acreages had a lot of forest on them in Red Creek, much of the land not ideal for crops or orchards, so they left the thick brush, where kids often played, and teenagers went to smoke weed or to drink stolen beers from their dad's garages.

Cliff passed by the fields on either side, a thin slice of prime land before the creek running through the heavy forest. It was somewhere around here, the Hendersons said, they saw the man. He wondered what kind of people got up for walks at six in the morning on a Sunday, and he supposed they were probably better people than he was.

As if on cue, he came upon the man. He was passed out, leaning against a thick tree trunk, clothes tattered and dried drool on his chin. There was something familiar about him, but he for sure wasn't a local. Cliff knew almost everyone, especially the drunks.

The guy had brown hair. Even through the mess, Cliff could tell his haircut wasn't done at the local Shear Delight on Main. Red plaid shirt, expensive-looking brown oxfords, and designer jeans. This guy looked like a rich man trying to fit in. Cliff was an old sheriff in a dingy town, but his aptitude at deduction hadn't faltered over the years.

With his foot, he nudged the guy. "Hey, sailor. Time to get up. Maybe get some water, have a shower." The guy didn't move, and Cliff noticed the lacerations. His hands were cut up, and his face was lined with small cuts, also bruised in a few places.

"Come on, buddy, let's wake up." He crouched down, keeping his distance while lightly slapping the man's stubbled cheek. He groaned and followed it up with a cough before blinking his red eyes open.

***

*P*aul's head fiercely ached, and his eyes took a few seconds to focus on the man kneeling before him. Panic set in and he thought he was under attack. Moving his arms slowly to cover his face, he tried to stand up. "Leave me alone!" he yelled, not sure where he was or why he was sitting in pain. Had he been mugged in Central Park?

"Whoa, fella, take it easy," the man said in a hoarse voice. Paul could now see he was in a beige uniform: a policeman, but not NYPD. Then it came back to him. He was in Red Creek.

"Where am I?" he asked, still sitting down. The cop stood up, giving him his hand. He clasped it, letting the older man take the brunt of his weight. Paul's head swam as he straightened and leaned against the tree.

"In the trees behind the fields off Wood Street. Can you tell me what you're doing out here?" the cop asked.

Paul couldn't remember. "It's embarrassing, but I don't know."

"That's not a great answer. What's your name?" the cop asked, tapping his foot, either impatiently or nervously.

"Paul. Paul Alenn," he said through the cotton in his mouth.

The man's eyes widened for a split second and quickly went back to normal. If Paul didn't know better, the guy knew him, which wasn't surprising, since his family had been residents there for forty years.

"You remember me? Sheriff Cliff?" the officer asked.

The name seemed vaguely familiar. "I think so. It's been a long time since I've been in town."

"Where are you staying?" he asked Paul.

They were walking now, back toward the street. The sheriff didn't seem to be too worried about him, and they casually strode side by side.

"On Wood Street." Paul kept the conversation simple while he racked his memory for anything after walking back last night. He was drawing a blank. He'd been fairly drunk, but not "pass out in the woods" drunk. Then he recalled the shadowed form, and his memory stopped there.

"You okay there, sport? Nose is a little…" the sheriff said, pointing to his own lip.

Paul wiped his face, and blood came back with his hand.

"Yeah, something about the country air, I think," Paul replied, trying to cover up the strange situation.

"Is it the country air that gave you those lacerations on your face? Or that bruise on your cheek?" Cliff asked, leading Paul to run his hands over his face.

"I was in a fight last night." He explained the altercation with Jason at the bar to the older man. Cliff grunted, nodding his head along with the story.

"That doesn't really explain the small cuts all over you."

Paul noticed the slices on his hands, and when he ran his fingers over his forehead, there were slight line indents, almost scabbed over already. What the hell had happened to him last night?

They made their way out of the forest area, now walking between the harvested fields. The morning sun was blinding, and Paul's head pounded from a mixture of whiskey and the punch to the face. What he really wanted was a steaming hot shower, a cup of coffee, and a couple pills for the pain.

"I really don't know how I got them. I suppose I was hit harder than I thought by Jason. Must have had a concussion. Really feels like it right now. I must have stumbled into the brambles and cut myself up on the thick underbrush. I remember getting some serious scratches from them as a kid playing out there." Paul nodded back toward the trees.

"Sure. Sure. I can see how that might have happened.

Well, the Hendersons called it in, so I'll let them know nothing malicious was going on," the sheriff said.

"The Hendersons? The ones a couple houses down from my mom's?" Paul asked, thinking about the very old frail woman who used to live there.

"I imagine they're one and the same. He's the grandson of the old coot who would have been there when you were a kid."

They made it to the sidewalk, and Paul could almost feel his headache lessen as soon as both feet were off the path and onto the concrete.

The cruiser was parked there, cherries flashing, drawing unwanted attention to them. What a homecoming. First morning there, and he was being escorted home looking like he'd been in a hellish battle. A woman's face peered through a window at him, quickly pulling the curtain over herself as he made eye contact. Quite the spectacle.

"I'm up here. I think I can make it now." Paul wanted nothing more than the man to leave him alone.

"No car here?" Cliff asked.

"Left it at the bar last night. Not safe to drink and drive."

The old man nodded and made a grunting noise. "Okay, see that you get into your own bed tonight, Mr. Alenn. Hey, you're that author, right?" he asked.

Paul thought he might explode if he didn't get inside his old house's door, and soon. "Yep. Want an autograph?" he asked, laughing lightly.

"Nope. Not much of a reader myself. Going to be in town long?"

Paul could tell the man was goading him into something, but he wasn't going to play along. "A few days, until the house is up for sale. Don't worry, you won't see my mug again while I'm here," he assured the man, hoping he was right.

"All right. Take care, Mr. Alenn." With that, Paul was alone on the sidewalk. By the time he made it to the door and unlocked it, the cruiser was driving by slowly. The sheriff rolled by at no more than five miles an hour and gave him the same hard stare he had when Paul had first driven by him yesterday afternoon. Now he knew it had been the same man.

The house door closed, and he leaned his back against it after locking the deadbolt. Welcome back to Red Creek.

***

"You sure know how to make an entrance, big brother. One night, and you get decked and kicked by your old best friend, and you get escorted home by the local authorities. God, I hate that Cliff bastard. All he does is sit around, eating fast food and giving tickets for nothing. He gave Darrel three citations last year alone." Beth wiped his face with antiseptic wipes, the alcohol stinging each and every little cut like torture.

"I didn't plan it like that. I don't even put my characters through this much abuse," he said, knowing that wasn't true. Some of the things they had to go through would have killed him long ago. Lucky for Paul, the supernatural underworld wasn't really after him.

"Well, that should do it. They don't look too bad, and none of them are very deep, so you should heal up quickly. I don't think you should go back there again." Beth had an obvious worried look across her face. If there was one thing about Beth that Paul knew, she couldn't hide her emotions.

"I don't plan on it." The clock read eleven AM, and his

stomach was growling. "Did I smell food when you first came in?" he asked.

She smiled. "I forgot all about that when I saw your face. I brought breakfast from Chuck's."

Soon he was wolfing down a breakfast sandwich, guzzling a cup of coffee alongside it. Beth slowly ate, and he forced himself to stop eating so fast and not act like such a Neanderthal. She probably had enough of that at home.

He had every intention of spending some time writing while he was in Red Creek, and so far, it was nothing like the quiet getaway he'd hoped for. They really needed to get to packing the house up.

"Let's stick to the plan today. I think we can get the rest of the upstairs done if we put our minds to it." Paul would then spend the evening staying inside, sipping decaf and writing his book. He was right at a crucial moment in the plot, and the outline for the next act was bursting to get out of his head and onto the computer.

"And then dinner over at my house, right?" she asked, setting down the last half of her sandwich.

Paul had forgotten about the promise he'd made yesterday. He grasped for an excuse, but none of them made him sound like anything but a jerk. He considered telling her that his head hurt too much, but Beth was someone he really didn't want to lie to. "Of course. Now, how about we get to it?"

Four hours later, and Paul was opening the living room windows as the temperature inside warmed alongside the abnormally hot fall day. Beth found an oscillating fan and it rotated back and forth, blowing warm air around the living room. Stacks of boxes lined the walls, and old furniture sat in the same spots they'd been in for almost forty years.

"Darrel said he'll come and help move the big stuff tomorrow. We have a truck rented, and the Salvation Army store a couple towns over is expecting the load Tuesday. Sound good?" Beth was sweating, and Paul was delighted when he found the six-pack of cold ones in the fridge. He cracked two of them, noting how quickly the condensation dripped down them and onto the coffee table in the heat.

"You sure you should be drinking? I mean, you were woken up in the forest this morning by the sheriff and have unaccounted-for injuries, all after trying to keep up with Jason Benning. The guy is half whiskey at this point." Beth may have judged him, but she took a heavy swallow of the lager, audibly smacking her lips afterwards.

"Don't say that about Jason. How would you feel if Isabelle went missing?" As soon as the words seeped out of his mouth, he regretted saying them. Before she could reply, he tried to recover. "That would be terrible. I'm sure everyone liked Jason before Isaac went missing, right?"

She nodded, taking another swig of beer. "You're right. I should cut him a break." Her cell buzzed on the table, and a picture of her husband appeared on the screen. He was in a suit, and Paul guessed it was the one time in two years he'd worn one, so she kept it as her contact image for him, to remind herself he could clean himself up once in a while.

Swiping the phone, she answered. "Whoa, hold on. Tommy O'Brian? Are they sure? Where? We're almost done here for the night, so we'll be right there to help with the search." She hung up, leaving Paul confused by her rapid conversation with her husband. Beth chugged the rest of the bottle and wiped her mouth, tears building up in her eyes. "He's missing."

"Who's missing?" Paul asked, his heart pumping hard in his chest.

"Tommy O'Brian. His kid sister is Isabelle's best friend. They found his bike over by the creek across town.

I guess he's been gone since last night." Beth was already reaching for her purse.

Paul's stomach dropped. He'd heard about the kids disappearing around here but didn't think he'd be in town to witness it happen. He suddenly wished for his townhouse in New York and a simpler time when Terri and Taylor had still been by his side. He left his beer untouched and grabbed his keys and wallet.

"Can you take me to my car first?" he asked.

Seven

*T*he sun was almost down, casting massive shadows of decades-old trees among the fields where the search party was congregated. Paul's shoes were covered in canola husk, and he stood beside his niece Isabelle as she solemnly waved at her friend Bianca from thirty yards away.

"We'll find him, Isabelle," Beth said, trying to sound convincing, but Paul didn't think the little girl was buying it. There were probably too many rumors about the school yards, monsters created by kids' imaginations to explain the disappearances over the years.

"What do you think, Uncle Paul?" she asked, her voice strong.

"I think your mom's right." Paul didn't want to contradict her with the facts. It probably was a monster – not one that went bump in the night, but a sick, perverted human version, seeking prey that was weaker than itself. He thought of Jason and knew he would stop at nothing to find out the truth, no different than if Paul lost Taylor in a similar circumstance.

"We're going to spread out in ten-yard spaces, combing every inch of this field from here to the creek. Another group is going to be in the forest on the other side of the river. It'll be a little more treacherous over there in the dark, so please volunteer if you're up for it and are sure-footed," a woman in a deputy's uniform called out, her voice loud enough to not need a loudspeaker.

"Beth, I'll go on the other side. I spent a lot of time over there; I think I'd be of more use," Paul said.

"That was twenty years ago. I'd rather you stayed with us," Beth said.

Darrel was there, hands thrust so deep into his pockets, Paul thought he would push through them. "I'll go with your brother. You stay here with Belle and walk the line. Give me a chance to catch up with the guy." His voice was light enough, but Paul saw a hard look in his eyes, and instantly knew it was a bad idea. He couldn't quite raise his concern to them.

"Fine, but play nice," she said, and the ladies followed the uniformed officer as Paul and Darrel headed for the creek.

"There's a bridge ahead a ways. It's seen better days, but we can cross there," Darrel said, and Paul remembered the bridge. It was put up in ninety-six after some kids fell in trying to cross. The river was only five yards wide at this point, but five yards was the Grand Canyon to a middle school kid trying to jump it on a BMX.

"How are things, Darrel? I was looking forward to seeing you tonight, though I thought it would be at your kitchen table, not scouring the forest," Paul said as they neared the creek, which was flowing faster than he remembered.

"Is this a joke to you?" Darrel asked.

"Of course not." Paul got the idea anything he said tonight was going to be wrong. He had to err on the side of caution. "Look, I know you don't like me, and frankly, I don't blame you. I've never been around, and other than sending Isabelle a few presents, I've been a lousy uncle. I've always been a shitty brother–" He paused, meaning the words he was struggling to get out. "–and a crappy brother-in-law too."

They walked a few steps in silence, approaching the bridge that wasn't more than two four-by-eights with two-by-fours nailed to it, straddling the rocky water bed.

"And all of the sudden, that's all going to change?" Darrel asked with more than a twinge of doubt in his voice. "You're gonna roll into town, make Beth think you're back in her life for good, then disappear for another twenty years?"

Paul stopped before the half-rotted wooden bridge, turning to his brother-in-law. He'd always seen Darrel as kind of a fool, but this man was anything but. He cared about Beth fiercely, Paul could see it now. He was the bad guy, not Darrel, and he was trying to protect his wife.

"She idolizes you, you know. She's never spoken a bad word about you. She's always blamed your mother for you leaving and not coming back, not you. Every book you write, even if the rest of the world says it's crap, she devours over and over, trying to keep a piece of you close to her. If you break her heart..." Darrel stopped talking, but Paul knew where he was going with it. "Don't come back ever again if you do." He stalked away from Paul, boots stomping on the dangerous-looking bridge. It swayed under the weight, and Paul followed him across, knowing he would get wet if he fell through, nothing more.

The words he'd just heard cut through him like a knife. He pictured Beth snuggled up in her living room, a blanket on, candles burning, drinking a cup of decaf late at night while Darrel snored away in bed and Isabelle dreamed of fairies and unicorns. A worn-out paperback of *The Underneath* was in her hand, and from the looks of the spine, she'd read it a dozen times. He could see her eyes tighten at a tense scene, or her toes wriggle when the Shadows emerged for the final battle.

"I love her, you know," Paul said. "She can't only blame my mother. I've had a block about coming back to Red Creek for years. Every time I want to, I feel sick, nauseous. Terri tried countless times, and I couldn't do it. It was one of the things on her lengthy list of my failures as a husband, and as a human, I suppose." It was strange opening up to someone about it, especially this man he hardly knew.

"I know you think I'm some hillbilly or whatever, but your roots are here too, Paul. Maybe you and I aren't so different." Darrel turned from him, and they walked to the group of ten people forming a circle. They stepped aside, and Sheriff Cliff was standing there with a clipboard.

"Mr. Alenn, I'm surprised to see you here. Darrel, good to see you," the gruff man said. His uniform was still wrinkled, and Paul thought he could smell booze in the air. If you'd seen as many missing persons over the years as Cliff, the bottle probably went hand in hand with the job.

They went over the map of the area. The fields ran for miles between the town and the creek, this direction. East a mile, the creek turned south, and cut through the far side of town. Forest lined the creekside on the north side, and that was where they were headed. West along the creek, until they passed the area Paul had found himself in that very morning. It was about a three-mile walk, and in the dark, the forest bed could be hazardous, according to Cliff, who wasn't shy about saying it three or four times before he was done.

Paul caught a glimpse of the map and saw a massive red area marked off a couple miles north of them.

"What's there?" he asked, trying to remember from being a kid. He was sure he and Jason would have explored it as trouble-seeking teens.

"Everyone knows that. It hasn't changed since you

were a kid, Mr. Alenn." The sheriff stared hard at Paul, conveying a secret message between the two of them that Paul didn't understand. "It's Granny Smith's Orchard."

Paul recalled Jason mentioning it the night before. He pictured the blonde woman in her skin-tight jeans. Fumbling in his back pocket, he slipped out the business card, being careful no one saw him. *Katherine Smith, Marketing Director.* He slid it back into the pocket, unsure why he still had that on him. He'd toss it in the trash when he got home. Home. He almost laughed at himself, calling his old house *home.*

"Granny Smith's is the end point for tonight's search, so we have this square to search. Everyone good? Grab a flashlight and a radio." Cliff pointed to a box, and one by one, they grabbed a light and a cheap electronics-store radio. Cliff made sure they were all set to the same frequency, and they were off in pairs. With the dark coming, he thought teaming up would be the best bet, especially if someone dangerous was behind it. Paul looked to the other group, still walking away down the field in a straight line. A couple German shepherds, probably borrowed from the closest city's police force, walked with police officers, not sheriffs. Reinforcements were a good thing. He spotted the back of Beth and Isabelle and looked for Jason, but didn't see him. Maybe it was too soon after searching countless days for his own son, or maybe he hadn't heard about the missing kid.

They tested their radios, one for each duo of searchers, and when they were all working, they set out. Paul and Darrel were relegated to the north section, so they walked straight up, away from the creek for a mile and a half, the forest not that thick on the way. They didn't speak much, other than some direction conversation, and when they arrived at a spot they could see the lights of the orchard's main house from, they stopped, turning west.

"Guess this is about as far as we go," Darrel said, starting to take long steps, reminding Paul of a toy soldier.

"How many of these search parties have you been on?" Paul asked, trying to catch up to the taller man.

Darrel grunted. "Think this is five or six over the years."

"And always children? How can that be? I mean, if it's some pervert out here, shouldn't they have found him by now? How many houses are in this area we're searching?" Paul pushed out the questions.

"Only around ten houses. Mostly old farmhouses. Think there's one coming up in a half mile or so. And no, not only kids. Probably another ten adults have disappeared, but most of them were assumed to have been killed by animals. A couple were found a few years back, ripped apart. Wolves, they said." Darrel didn't slow as he talked. Both of their flashlights scanned the ground ahead of and beside them as they walked, hoping for a sign of anything.

"Animals? Really? Does anyone believe that?"

"Nope."

"What do you think it is?"

"If I were a betting man, which I am once a month at Chuck's poker game, I'd say we have a real psycho on our hands," Darrel answered. "Must be getting old, though."

"Why do you say that, Darrel?"

"Well, if he was killing people back when you were a kid, and he's still doing it, then he has to be getting up there." Darrel stopped, shining his flashlight at Paul's face. Paul squinted and stuck his hand out to stop the blinding light.

He racked his brain, trying to understand what he was hearing. Killing people when he was a kid? He had no memory of anything like that going on while he lived in

Red Creek.

"What the hell are you talking about?" he asked. Darrel's face seemed to droop in the moonlight.

"Forget it," he said, and kept walking.

"Wait a second. I don't remember anything like that going on." Paul tripped on something and looked down, ready to curse a tree root. His flashlight cast an LED glow on something white.

He leaned over, ready to pick it up, when Darrel yelled at him. "Stop! Don't touch it. That's a shoe. It could be his." The click of a radio sounded, and Paul stood up, continuing to shine the light on the kid's sneaker. In the dark forest, he could make out a smear on the side of the shoe, a red splash on the white leather.

***

*T*erri swirled the cup in light circles, the latte foam splashing on the wooden table. Taylor sat beside her, a bored look etched across her usually affable face.

Don Bronstein was showing Paul's place… *their* place, and they'd been booted to the streets for the day. The good news was, she finally found out where her husband was. At first, she thought Don must be wrong, maybe trying to pull her leg, but he assured her, Paul was in Red Creek. His cell phone was going straight to voicemail, and after leaving one message, she didn't want to seem over-excited to talk to him, though her number would probably show up half a dozen times on his missed call list.

She'd even tried Beth's house, where some babysitter mentioned a story about a search team. She decided to call the kid's bluff and Google the town.

She sipped her drink, reminded of how much better

the coffee shops were in New York. LA couldn't hold a candle to it. The results popped up, and she clicked NEWS to quicken the search. It had happened that day, so the majors hadn't picked anything up, but there were some bulletins from local papers' sites, talking about a missing boy named Tommy O'Brian.

"Mommy, is Grandpa going to be okay?" Taylor asked, worry thick in her voice. Maybe the pouting wasn't because of boredom; maybe she was concerned.

"He is. The surgery went well, but he has a long road ahead of him." The bypass had been a success, but he wasn't out of the woods yet, they'd told her.

Her thoughts shot back to Paul, amazed he could go back to Red Creek. She'd tried getting him to face those demons for years, and here he was, searching for a missing kid in his old hometown. The whole scenario was exactly like the one Paul's mother had told her about years ago, and something in her gut told her it was bad news.

"Taylor, what do you say about going to see Daddy in his old home?"

She lit up like a streetlight at the prospect.

"Yeah!" Taylor said, a genuine smile covering her face for the first time in a couple days.

"We'll leave after seeing Grandpa tomorrow."

Eight

*O*f all the people to find evidence of the missing boy, it was that Alenn kid. Maybe he wasn't so much a kid as he was a man reaching his middle years, but Cliff would always remember pulling him from that building all those years ago. The whole story pissed him off so much, he pushed it back down. Maybe he should have gone to see that shrink when they'd offered it to him, but Reilly had been such a bastard, he hadn't wanted to talk about what he'd seen to anyone. The threat on his job had been enough for Cliff to clam up, and he still didn't want to open up about it.

Everyone had demons to deal with, Cliff among them. Paul's vicious tale back then was unbelievable, and the cover-up by Reilly was unforgivable. But in the end, everyone went on with their lives, and the kids stopped disappearing, at least for a few years. What was past, was past.

He shook his head as he slipped on the gloves, bagging the shoe. Tommy's parents were there, mother howling like a wolf at the moon, and the father holding his sobbing wife, a grim look of despair across his face.

Paul hung around behind the group like a scared animal. His niece was standing with him, chatting away. Her uncle had a distant look, and Cliff doubted he was hearing a word of the conversation. He didn't blame the guy. He wondered how much Paul recollected of that time, because he didn't seem to remember any of it at all. He surely didn't recall the now-sheriff.

"Cliff, what do we do now?" Gloria was beside him, her usual boisterous voice a quiet whisper.

His head throbbed, and he wanted nothing more than to call it a night. But there could be more evidence, so they kept at it, combing the area more thoroughly, utilizing all the people in the search party. They kept at it until four AM, until everyone was all but frozen and sleeping on their feet.

Something about seeing the Alenn kid and the community support was giving Cliff the sustenance he needed. He might be cynical, but maybe it was time to take his head out of the sand. He was going to find Tommy and make this end for good.

***

*T*he light was seeping from the edges of the closed curtains in his old room when Paul lay down for bed that morning. He was exhausted. Seeing that blood-splattered shoe made everything so real. He'd come to help tidy up a house and couldn't help but feel like he'd been thrown into a whole new world, one that part of his brain was finding familiar. He felt a drive to find this kid, to help bring closure to Jason, and somehow to himself too.

He drifted away slowly, his body shutting down, even though his mind was racing a mile a minute. And he dreamt.

The air was warm, feeling like a day only can in the dog days of summer. It was one where you could go out at five in the morning in shorts and a tank top, and already start sweating. Jason told him to bring some cans, so he loaded his denim backpack full of his dad's beer cans from the recycle bag.

His mom smiled at him from the window, giving him a quick wave. She'd packed some sandwiches for the two boys, and a couple of juice boxes. She rarely let him go into the forest without something to eat, because God forbid he blow a tire and need to walk back.

Hopping onto his bike, he started to pump his legs, getting some speed right off the bat. The canola fields emanated smells in the heat, and he sneezed as he approached them, wiping his nose with his left arm. The path was packed down from so many rides over it. Jason would be in their favorite spot in the trees, and if he wasn't lying to Paul, he'd have his older brother's BB gun. This was going to be so awesome.

Paul shifted in the bed, sweat beading on his forehead as he fitfully slept.

Jason wasn't there when he showed up at their spot. Paul found a downed log, pulling out the cans one by one and lining them up on the bark. He hoped he would be a better shot than Jason. His friend was better at everything else; the least the universe could do was let him shoot better than the athletic guy.

An hour passed, and Paul paced around the copse before sitting down at the base of a tree. Half a sandwich went down, and he wiped his forehead with a napkin from the lunch bag. It was mid-afternoon, and the heat was growing. Wafts of warm canola and apples from the orchards north of him clung to his nose as he sat, starting to get angry at his missing friend. He closed his eyes.

When they opened, it was dark, sweat slick on his body. The sudden change was jarring, and Paul felt the same as he did after seeing a late-night scary movie and being sent to get something from the basement freezer. Something was watching him.

"Jason? Is that you?" he called, his voice strained after not speaking for a few hours. His nose was running, and he cursed his allergies, but when he wiped it with the napkin, it came back dark. It was bleeding. His pulse raced as he stood, and he kept the napkin to his still-flowing nostril, ready for a full-blown panic. He spun around, looking for a bike that wasn't there. Where had he left it? He was

sure it was right beside him when he sat down.

Deciding to run, he tried to identify which direction would take him home. In the dark, under the canopy of leaves, he couldn't tell north from south. Panic rose in his throat, his knees nearly gave out, and when he saw it, he picked a path to run.

At first, he only heard the branches breaking as something stepped near him, and that was when he noticed there were no other sounds. No cows mooing in the distance, no birds chirping in the trees; only the crickets from the farm pond a mile away. Another branch cracked on the forest bed, this time closer. He froze, a scream caught in his dry throat as he turned to see it.

A shadow loomed ten feet from him, a thick shape, black as the devil's heart, arms hanging at its sides lazily, its head moving from side to side slowly, as if assessing its prey. He finally found his voice and yelled at the top of his lungs before turning away from the thing and running as fast as he could. He could hear it following him, not nearly as fast as he expected. He could get away!

Paul was running out of breath, but his legs kept pumping. He could see the path that would lead him home through the thick tree trunks. Almost there... his foot caught something, probably a surface root he was always warned to be wary of. He hit the ground hard. Spinning to his back, he saw it again, looming back a few feet. He screamed again, this time for his mom, but it was cut off as the thing was over top of him and all went black.

Paul lurched up in his old twin bed, panting heavily. He touched his face and scanned the room, looking for the shadow, but it was just him, safely awake from whatever horrible nightmare that was. It had felt so real, so vivid. That wasn't a memory of his, but deep down, it could have been. There was something vaguely familiar about it, but in the dream, he loved his mom and had called for her. Wasn't there a time they were so close he'd cry when he went to school? She had always packed him sandwiches, but then something changed one day, and he couldn't put a finger on when, or why.

The old alarm clock's red lighting glared the time at him. One in the afternoon. He'd been out for hours, but it only felt like a few minutes. His head throbbed, so he headed to the bathroom, seeking out some pain medication. At that point, anything would do.

The medicine cabinet was half-full of pill bottles. He saw some were labeled for his father, who'd been gone for years. Heart meds, he guessed. He fumbled through more little orange bottles, his family name on all of them. An assortment of pills for his mother – all well past expiration dates, it seemed – were all stuffed onto the small glass shelves. Her new stuff was probably organized in those daily pill dispensers, overseen by Beth.

When he'd given up hope of actually finding anything over the counter, he spotted some anti-inflammatories only a year past expiration. That would have to do. A lone jar sat behind it, his own name printed on the side. The date was from the nineties, and he cringed at how his mother could keep everything. Picking it up, he shook it, feeling only a couple capsules banging around inside. Clozapine. He had no idea why his name was on them, but he pocketed the pills, feeling a mystery he wasn't sure he wanted to solve popping up.

His phone rang from the bedroom, and he slipped two of the regular pills in his mouth, slurping some water out of the faucet. He dashed to the bedside table, seeing Beth's name across the screen. "Hello," he answered.

"Hey, Paul. You up?" she asked.

"Nope. I'm sleeping and yet still talking to you. It's a skill I have." He thought a joke might shake the cobwebs of terror still lingering from his dream. It didn't.

"Hardy har har. Look. Isabelle won't let me leave today, and I was supposed to go see Mom. Is there any chance you'd maybe…" She stopped, probably hoping Paul would interject before she had to say it. He didn't, so she continued. "Maybe you could go in my place?"

He couldn't go see her. Could he? It had been so long, and the anger and resentment was all but burned out at seeing her sad life in boxes back in their old house. The dream was horrible, but the feeling he had waving to his mom, and being there in the summer as a kid, was strong. He longed for it suddenly.

"She probably won't even be lucid. She rarely is anymore." Beth was trying to sell it, and a week ago, Paul might have preferred seeing a catatonic woman in her place, but he wanted to see her: his mom from years ago, when she was pleasant, and fun, and loving.

"I'll do it," he said, hoping he wasn't going to regret those words in an hour.

Beth squealed. "Thank you! I think it'll be good for you guys."

"Any word on Tommy?" Paul asked. Beth would know if there was any news.

"Nothing more. They're talking to all the farmers again, but it's the same old story. You coming for dinner tonight, since it got pushed yesterday?" she asked.

"What time?" he asked, his stomach already growling.

"Make it five," she said, and he could almost hear her smile. It made him grin widely.

"See you soon," he said, hanging up.

It was two thirty when he pulled into the Greenbriar parking lot. The building looked like it had undergone some new renovations. He remembered it being called something different, and back then, it was a senior residence, not an assisted-living facility. From the size of the place, it would be the only one within a few towns' distance, so they would all funnel their loved ones to Red

Creek.

It was Monday afternoon, and the lot was nearly empty except for the staff parking along the building, which was mostly full. The Greenbriar sign on the building stared at him as he got out of his car, causing him to wish he'd stayed at the house and packed up. The sooner he got the house sold, the sooner he could get out of Red Creek. But to where? Don would probably sell his townhouse in a week. Then what was he going to do?

With reservations, he took one footstep after another, until he was standing at the reception desk inside. A middle-aged woman ignored him from her seat, her brown hair streaked with gray, her uniform wrinkled and stained. This didn't give him confidence in the place. The old adage "you only get one chance at a first impression" floated to the forefront of his mind, and instead of saying something curt, he decided to play happy.

"Hi there. I hope you're having a nice day," he said, and she finally looked up, peering at him from behind thick bifocals. She had that "what are you selling?" look in her eyes. "Hello–" He scanned and caught her name on the tag pinned to her ample chest. "–Marcia. I'm here to see Helen Alenn. Can you point me in the right direction?"

She stared blankly at him, a slight frown on her excessively made-up forehead. "And who are you?" she asked, a hint of suspicion in her tone.

"I'm her son."

"Didn't know she had a son. She's in two-eleven, but you're going to need an orderly to go in with you. Hold tight a moment." She grabbed the phone and spun around, whispering into the receiver.

A minute later, a large man wearing white pants and a short-sleeved white button-up shirt appeared. "Ben, would you please show Mr. Alenn to his mother's room?" she asked sweetly, winking at the orderly. Paul didn't think he was supposed to catch that interaction out of the corner of his eye.

"You got it, Marcia. Right this way." The man lumbered down the hall, and Paul trudged along behind him, hands sweating at the idea that he was soon going to be face to face with his mom, a woman he hadn't seen or spoken to in so long.

They arrived at the room, and Ben knocked before swinging the door open. He stepped aside, giving Paul a view of the cramped space. An elderly woman sat in a retro chair, staring out a barred window.

"Sorry, this isn't my mom," Paul whispered, and noticed Ben was sauntering down the hall.

He was about to leave, when he saw the picture frame set up on her nightstand. It was his family, circa 1993, Beth a little girl in a fluorescent orange dress and tights. Dad was standing in the back, his one suit on, with a tie Paul had bought him for Father's Day the year before. Mom sat on a stool, flanked by her two kids. She looked pretty in the picture, and he could almost remember the day, this many years later.

"Mom?" Paul asked, taking a small step into the room.

She turned slowly to him, and she looked like she'd aged forty years, not twenty, but he could see it was her in the eyes. They widened as she took him in, before she looked from Paul to the picture beside her.

"Paul?" she asked, her voice familiar yet distant.

His eyes filled with tears and he rushed over to the frail woman, kneeling on the ground by the chair and enveloping her in a strong hug, his head buried into her neck. Her cool hand landed on the back of his neck, and she stroked his hair. They stayed like that for at least a minute before Paul pulled away.

His mom's eyes were clear, and a smile showed her teeth, like she did when she was actually happy.

"I'm so sorry, Mom. Sorry for all of it. I'm glad to see you now."

"It's not your fault. None of it was. Remember that, Paul. I did what I had to do. Sheriff Oliver, Dr. Norman… we had no choice." The words made no sense, but she was looking at him, sure of her words.

"I don't understand what that means. We just didn't get along. I wish I'd been a better man and come back sooner."

Her eyes were distant now, like they were out of focus, and she turned away, looking out the window. "Is he taking them again?"

"Is he taking what?"

"Not what. Who."

He was more confused and asked the other question. "Is he taking whom?"

"The children," she said in a whisper.

Dread raced down Paul's spine and to his feet. "What are you talking about?"

She looked back to him, smiling once again. "Hello, Ben. Is it time for dinner?"

"Mom, it's me. Paul, your son." He fought the urge to shake her.

"Don't be silly. I don't have a son. Come, take me to the dining room." She stretched her arm out for him to grab and help her up.

Maybe if he stayed with her, she'd return to the clarity she'd had a moment ago. He had so many questions to ask her, starting with the dream and the pill bottle in his pocket, not ending with the question she posed to him. Maybe it was all the ramblings of a woman with dementia, but there was more to it than that, he was sure.

He led her down the hall, leaving the wheelchair from the room behind. She seemed to be doing a fair enough job, but they were moving slowly. When had she gotten so old? He'd missed so much, and she'd missed so much of his life too. As they sat at a table, muzak humming through some cheap speakers, he regretted many things.

He stayed another hour, sitting making small talk with the shell of his mom, wishing he could have a real conversation with her, but feeling bad for being selfish about it. Eventually, she asked him to help her back, saying she was tired. She called him Ben a few times, never realizing he was Paul other than that first minute together. He swore he'd try again tomorrow.

Paul left Greenbriar around four and decided to pick up a bottle of wine for dinner. The liquor store was the same one he'd snuck into with a fake ID back in high school. It may have even been the very same old guy behind the counter, who'd checked his obvious fake back then, but grunted when Paul had plopped his twenty down. He felt like he might get carded again when he approached the guy, but his three-day growth of graying beard probably wouldn't warrant a second glance.

As he turned to leave, two greasy men walked in the store, chimes jingling as the door swung open, then closed. They looked Paul in the eye, and the left one spit a wad of chewing tobacco mess on the floor beside him. *Keep it classy, Red Creek.*

"That your car out there?" the guy with an old trucker hat asked.

Paul looked out the window, seeing his was the only car in the lot. "Excuse me, guys," he said, moving for the door, past Red Creek's finest.

The one who'd spit stuck a lanky arm out to stop him, but Paul stopped before he could be touched by the gap-toothed mouth breather.

"What exactly are you after here, fellas?" Paul asked, trying to sound more confident than he felt. They didn't look like much, but there were two of them, and they seemed to have a bee in their bonnet about something.

"Mr. Fancy Pants rolls into town in his fancy car, and all of a sudden, we have ourselves a missing little boy. Do you like little boys, Mr. Fancy Pants?" the short one with the hat asked.

Paul's blood started to boil, and he saw red. The urge to grab a bottle of wine from the racks and club him over the head with it was hard to push down, but he tried to stay as calm on the outside as he could.

"I don't know who the hell you guys think you are, but I'm leaving." He pushed past them, and the tall one shoved him from behind. Paul almost lost his footing but caught himself and barged through the exit.

They opened the door behind him and shouted at him. "We know what you did. Remember, we'll be watching you." They started to laugh and went back into the liquor store.

Paul's heart pounded, not from fear of being in a fight, but that he'd had to stop himself from trying to kill those guys. In New York, he'd had his share of altercations on the streets, but he was good at avoiding eye contact with the tough guys and kept to himself. This time, he wanted nothing more than to leave a smear on the yellow linoleum inside.

By the time he was in the car and rolling down the street, his hands were still shaking. It wasn't until he was back at the house with the door closed behind him that he felt better. The stress of the visit so far was getting to him. It was as if one crazy event after the other was stacking up, and he was afraid he was about to topple.

Checking his phone, he noticed it was dead. He really needed a new one. This battery died far too fast. He plugged it in, leaving it on the kitchen counter, and changed his shirt to a sweater. The nights were coming faster and cooler since he'd come to Red Creek.

By the time he was done with that, it was time to head over to Beth's. He checked the phone, wondering if Don had called about the house yet, but it was only at five percent charged. With a groan, he left the cell on the counter and left, locking the door behind him.

The sunlight was waning, and he was thankful for the sweater as he made his way to the car. Something moving caught his attention down the street, and he saw a person running onto the path between the fields. His feet started to walk him that direction, his brain disconnecting from everything else. Before he knew it, he was standing there, staring forward but seeing nothing out of the ordinary. He briefly wondered if Tommy was out there somewhere, before snapping out of it. What was he doing? He was already late for dinner, and here he was, staring into space like his mother.

The idea her condition might be hereditary crossed his mind. With a last look toward the trees in the distance, he went back to his car and started it. When he looked up, a figure stood a way down the path, hard to see from the angle and in the low light. A streetlight shot on, its daylight sensor kicking in, and the figure disappeared from sight. Paul had the urge to go inside, pack up the rest of the junk in the house, and drive back home tonight.

He almost reached for his phone when he remembered it was inside, and Beth was waiting. He'd disappointed her his whole life, and he wasn't going to anymore. With grim resolve, he drove away, trying to forget the last five minutes – hell, the last two days – as he crossed the town. Red

Creek looked dirtier and more run-down in the dimming autumn evening, a cesspool of the unemployed and unemployable.

Signs were hammered into the ground on wooden spikes around town. *Curfew Eight PM: Red Creek Sheriff's Department.* That was new. Paul wondered if old Cliff himself had run around that afternoon, bashing them into the ground like a priest trying to kill a vampire. Ashes to ashes, dust to dust.

It was still a couple hours from curfew, and kids still rode around town on bikes, their parents walking slowly behind with bags full of chips and pop from the local convenience stores. The only thing convenient about them was the fact you could get diabetes and lung cancer from the same place. He reprimanded himself for his snooty city views, but not too hard. It was the kind of comment he would have said in front of Terri, and she would have chided him, but done so with a light slap on the arm and a smile.

He passed a park near Beth's house and slowed to the allotted speed of fifteen miles an hour. The adults all seemed to turn their heads to watch him pass, as if he was there to take their kids and steal their cigarettes. The place was getting stranger by the hour.

Beth's house sat in a cul-de-sac, tucked away near the end, with a large pie-shaped lot. He pulled up beside Darrel's truck and in front of the garage, remembering to grab the bottle of wine before heading for the door.

The flowers were dying, but her garden looked fantastic. He was proud of her, knowing their mother hadn't had much in the way of a green thumb. She must have picked it up on her own, which was a statement in itself.

Before he knocked, the door swung open, Isabelle rushing out to throw her arms around his waist in a big hug. "Uncle Paul, I'm so glad you came." She smiled a gap-toothed grin at him, and they made their way inside, Paul wishing he'd brought her a gift.

"Uncle Paul's here!" she called to the kitchen, and before her parents showed up, Paul slipped out his wallet, passing a twenty-dollar bill to his niece. He put his finger to his lips. "Shhhh. Don't tell your parents," he said, and she tucked it in her pants, whispered a "thank you,'" and ran away, presumably to hide it away in her room.

"Come on in," Beth said, stepping into the room with a tea towel draped over her arm. She looked so different from the little girl he still had in his mind when he thought of her.

Her house was nicely furnished; used stuff, but well-maintained. Darrel sat in what Paul could only assume was his chair, drinking a can of beer. A football game played on TV, and they greeted with the usual assortment of quiet awkward hellos and grunts.

"I see there's a new curfew around town," Paul said to Beth as he followed her into the kitchen. He smelled a chicken roasting in the oven and caught a glimpse of the garlic mashed potatoes. When was the last time he'd eaten a home-cooked meal like that? At least six months.

"Yeah, I saw the signs. No word on Tommy yet, but they're still searching the area this afternoon. I heard the O'Brians are angry they haven't extended the search onto Granny Smith's Orchard. I guess the owners aren't being cooperative and are playing the private property card. I suppose that means the sheriff needs a warrant or something, but this is Red Creek, not New York City. We're not prepared for this kind of thing." Beth glanced at the bottle he held under his arm, and he carried it to the island, raising an eyebrow to her. She seemed to understand and passed him a corkscrew, one of the old-style twist-and-pull ones he never used anymore.

"Hey, wasn't that the place Dad used to do deliveries for?" Paul asked, pouring the two of them half-full glasses of wine.

Beth paused, tapping her fingernail on the cutting board. "I think it was. He worked for a bunch of places over the years, but I'm sure he did work for them when we were younger. I wonder what happened. Why couldn't he hold a job?"

Paul wasn't sure. "How was Dad in the last few years before he passed?"

"He was reserved. He listened to Mom barking orders at him. I have to think they weren't in love, that's for sure." She looked briefly toward the living room and back, fast, as if she'd been caught airing her own marriage's dirty laundry for the town to see. Paul didn't let it register he'd seen the moment.

"I don't remember him always being like that. He used to play catch with me all the time. He'd watch my soccer games when I was a little guy, chasing bugs instead of the ball. I think some event happened and it changed them. I had a dream last night… well, this morning." Paul went on to tell her about the dream where he was chased by the shadow.

"It sounds like something out of one of your books. Is that how you come up with this stuff?" Beth asked, eyes wide at his descriptive retelling of the nightmare. It was still fresh in his mind and had been all day.

"No. I…" He wanted to tell her about his idea for *The Underneath*, that night in the alley on the way back to campus, but he couldn't. "I make it up. It felt so real, like it became a memory, not a dream. I don't know if that makes any sense," he said, sipping the wine. Beth drained the steaming vegetables and set them on a cork holder.

"I suppose, but I rarely remember any of my dreams. Maybe ask Jason about it."

Jason. He hadn't shown up in the dream. If it was a memory, perhaps his friend would know something about it. He reached for his cell phone, thinking to text him, but it was still back at the house. How did people get through life without them anymore?

Paul set the table, Isabelle coming in to help put the cutlery on, like she said she always did. Darrel came in after being called three or four times, and Isabelle grabbed him another can of beer, taking his old one, rinsing it out, and adding it to a growing pile in a bag on the pantry floor.

"Isabelle, can you say grace?" Beth asked, and Paul was surprised they prayed before eating. That was a habit their family had broken a long time ago. It worried him, all of the things he was recalling about their family, and how different they'd been to where they ended up.

"God bless this food we're about to eat. Bless Daddy, and keep him safe while he works tomorrow, and bless Mommy for all the things she does for our family." Paul sat between the two girls, holding Beth's and Isabelle's hands as they sat with closed eyes. He took a peek, and Darrel's eyes were wide open, waiting impatiently for something to eat. "And bless Uncle Paul for helping Gramma, and for spending time with us. In Jesus' name, Amen."

Paul was impressed with her aptitude for words and awareness of those around her. She was a lot like her mother, it seemed. He squeezed his niece's hand and said Amen with Beth before they started to eat.

They made small talk, but Darrel rarely chimed in unless prodded. Paul knew the man didn't like him there, but tried to not let it show. He made every attempt to be the fun-loving man he sometimes could play, but rarely felt like it. *Are you a nice man? No, but I play one on TV.* He almost laughed at his own inner dialogue but cut it short when Darrel frowned at him.

"Paul, a few of us are heading out tonight to keep looking for Tommy. You in?" Darrel's steel-gray eyes stared hard at Paul, begging him to say no so he could be further disappointed in his brother-in-law.

"I thought they were done for the day. Isn't it going to be a little late? And it's freezing out there tonight. Who's *we?*" Beth spouted out the barrage of questions and comments.

He looked annoyed again, turning slowly from her to looking back at Paul. "So what do you say?"

Paul felt something was off and hated to be pushed into anything he didn't know more about, but he had to show this town he was here to help. It was calling to him. Tommy was calling to him. The sight of the kid's sneaker with blood on the side flashed into his mind. He looked away from the intense gaze watching him and forked a piece of chicken off his plate.

"Sure. I'm glad to help," he said.

"Good. Very good." Darrel stood, pushing his empty plate inches forward, and left the room, but not before grabbing another beer.

Isabelle poked at her carrots, the left side of her face leaning on her hand. "Mom, can I go watch my show in my room?" She could probably sense the room's mood.

"Okay, honey. Maybe we can watch one together after I clean up." Isabelle perked up to that and ran out of the room smiling.

"Paul, be careful out there tonight. His friends can be... well, you know most of them. They haven't changed a lot. And Darrel's been sucking back beers for hours now," his sister said quietly.

"I'll drive us, and don't worry. I'll watch my back." Paul got up and helped Beth clear the table; soon the dishwasher was running and coffee was brewed. They chatted about nothing and everything for a half hour, before Darrel came in and said it was time to go. He tossed a plaid jacket at Paul. It smelled like cigar smoke and lumber, but Paul slipped it on, and the fit wasn't too bad.

"Have a good night, sis. Thanks for dinner. See you tomorrow? We're already way behind on the house," Paul said. Beth nodded to him, saying she would take the day off work at the bank again. Paul hoped they were okay with her taking the time off. He really didn't want her to lose her job because of anything he suggested.

"I can work on it, and you come over when you're done for the day," he said, and she solemnly agreed, her eyes thanking him.

Once outside, the bite of the night hit him, and he was thankful for the jacket. "I'll drive," he said, walking toward his car. Darrel stopped and snickered.

"Fine, but I need to grab something first."

Paul started the engine, turning the heat up, when Darrel opened the back door and slid a rifle onto the back-seat leather. "What the hell is that for?" Paul barked.

"That's for the poor sucker who took Tommy."

Paul wanted nothing more than to tell him to get the damned gun out of his car, but Darrel was right. Maybe they did need protection. The figure in his dream came to mind. Better safe than sorry.

Nine

A gurney went by, flanked by medical professionals pushing the double doors open, into an area off-limits to visitors. Terri stood to see if it was her father and relaxed slightly when she saw a bald middle-aged man.

"Mommy, I'm hungry," Taylor said, looking up from the game she was playing on her mom's cell phone.

Terri looked at the time on the phone. Ten o'clock at night. She cursed herself for not checking that earlier. She'd been so preoccupied with finding out if her father was going to live or die. The surgery had gone well the day before, but here he was, now on the verge of crossing over to the other side. Part of her was glad her mother had already passed, so she didn't have to see the love of her life on his deathbed, but they all seemed to go way too early.

The smells and sounds of the hospital were too much for Terri at that moment, reminding her of being at her mom's bedside as the cancer eventually won. She could almost feel her mom's small hand sitting in hers as the heart monitor went flat, a slow beep telling her what she already knew. What she'd known for months.

"Mom, are you crying?" Taylor asked, poking her in the arm with a finger.

Terri wiped her tired eyes and wished Paul were there with them. Her husband, who wouldn't answer his cell phone. She worried at that, worried that he saw her name come up and chose to ignore it, chose to ignore that she was reaching out to him in a time of need or vulnerability. But she had a hard time believing he would choose not to call about her father. Through all the differences Terri and Paul had had over the years, Paul and her father were good friends. Paul was the successful, handsome man Terri's dad had always wanted her to marry, and according to him, he couldn't have asked for a better son-in-law.

She took the phone back from Taylor, who was holding it silently, game done with as her stomach growled. She dialed Paul's number one more time, and it went straight to voicemail again.

"Damn it," she muttered. "Come on, honey. Let's see if the cafeteria has anything left."

Taylor took the lead, already knowing her way around the hospital's many levels. The lights were dim, and the halls were quiet at this time of night. Visiting hours were over; only the few like her, waiting for news on their loved ones, remained, with red eyes and puffy cheeks, slumping in uncomfortable chairs in waiting rooms. If Paul wanted to write a horror story, it was right here, in a hospital.

Terri kept moving one tired leg after another down the long hall, following Taylor, who was getting farther and farther ahead.

"Honey, slow down," she called down the now empty hall. Where had they gone? It looked like an unused corridor, and Terri chided herself for following her daughter on auto-pilot.

She squinted, and Taylor was out of sight.

***

*M*ommy was so slow sometimes, and Taylor was hungry.

No, she was starving. She'd seen it on a show in school, where the kids in Africa were so hungry that their bodies started to eat themselves. That was what she thought was happening to her at that very moment. Hadn't the cafeteria been down this way? She spun around, not seeing anyone, and for the first time, she noticed some of the lights were out. Only small ones on the wall were lit, casting strange shadows over everything.

Hospitals were strange, but she'd always felt okay in them. It was like a big doctor's office. She liked the doctor's office. They always gave her a sucker, and the lady at the desk was plump and smelled nice. Now the hospital was starting to scare her. Taylor called out, but no one answered, and she started to walk back the way she'd come, only it didn't look familiar. Where was her mom?

A boy back home said he saw a ghost in a hospital once. When Taylor told him that was stupid, he said it wasn't and that hundreds of people died there every week, so wouldn't there be ghosts? At that time, she'd nodded, thinking his logic was sound, but now it scared her half to death.

Her hands were trembling as she started to run. A door clicked closed a few feet away, and she followed it, hoping it was her mommy. The door was heavy, but she pushed it open, sliding through and into an empty patient room.

"Mommy?" she asked, her voice a tiny shaking whisper.

There was a small door where the toilet would be, and a bed surrounded by a curtain. Wondering if her mom was maybe too tired and wanted a nap, she reached for the cloth, pulling it to the side.

A shadow loomed on the other side of the bed. Twice her height, it stood straight, face too dark to make out. A hand reached for her, and Taylor swore shadows peeled off long fingers, like smoke off a sputtering candle.

She screamed and turned to run, getting caught in the curtain. She fell to the ground, tangled, and scrambled to get out.

***

*T*erri heard the scream and rushed down the hall, listening for another sign of which room it had come from. Something thumped nearby, and she opened a room door to see a lump twisting on the ground.

"Taylor?" she asked, running for the bump in the curtain.

"Mommy! Help me!" she called in a voice so full of terror, Terri could hardly believe it was coming from her little daughter.

Terri tried to calm her down and rolled her out of the curtain. Taylor rushed into her arms, holding her tighter than she'd ever held her before. Her girl was sobbing, screeching something about a shadow man, and Terri thought about Paul's books and the shadow people in them. Had Taylor somehow read *The Underneath*? Or had her new friends found out who her father was and told her about the scary things in the book?

Terri picked Taylor up, leaving the room and heading back out of the unused halls, back into civilization with lights and people. A nurse looked at her sidelong, but a screaming kid in a hospital was probably more common than it should be, and no one bothered to see if she needed anything. She didn't; she just wanted her daughter to calm down.

Every time she mentioned the shadow man, goosebumps rose on Terri's arms.

By the time they reached the cafeteria, Taylor had started to relax, her wide eyes full of tears.

"I want Daddy," she said matter-of-factly, like her father could protect her from whatever it was she thought she'd seen in the dark room.

"I do too," Terri whispered, too quietly for Taylor to hear her.

***

Chuck stood beside Tyler and Nick, the gang from the other night at O'Sullivan's, at the fence line of Granny Smith's Orchard. They'd met at Chuck's Diner and taken two vehicles, parking them as close as they could get down a dirt road. From there, they'd hiked the last quarter mile to the property line.

Jason was with them, making it a group of six.

"So what makes any of you guys think the orchard has anything to hide?" Paul asked as they were about to use powerful bolt cutters to open a hole in the wire fence.

"I used to work there doing security," Nick said in his tight black jacket, looking ever so much like a guy who'd work as a night guard somewhere. "They have a couple of old barns, and even an ancient cabin on the far north side. No one is supposed to live there, and it's pretty run down. We were told to never go near it. Orders from the top. Seemed a little fishy, if you ask me."

"Have you guys ever come out here before?" Paul looked at Jason, stopping before he mentioned his son going missing last year.

They shook their heads.

Paul had a bad and familiar feeling, but kept it under wraps. He wasn't about to be the big sissy who bailed as these guys stuck their necks out, breaking the law to find a missing kid. "Well, we going to do this?" he asked, hoping someone would say no, and they could go home.

"Hell yeah, we are," Darrel said, clipping the fence wire in a line straight down before doing the same horizontally at the top and bottom. Soon Nick was pulling it back, giving them an opening to climb through. Paul was last, and his jacket caught on the sharp cuts, ripping a piece of Darrel's loaned jacket. He cursed and piled through.

They each had flashlights, which were currently moving around randomly over the landscape. Lucky for them, the high moon was near full, and the clouds were sparse in the night sky. Stars littered the expanse. There was nothing like a fall night in the country, with no city light pollution cascading to the heavens. Paul's breath hung in the air as he stared upwards.

"Come on," Darrel said quietly, as if Paul was embarrassing him.

The grounds were mostly grass, and lines of trees covered the area, the apples already removed from them as the nights had started to bring frost with them. He could still smell them, though, like a soft reminder of what was, and would be again.

"Which way?" Chuck asked, and Paul thought he could see a little bit of a tremble in the man's hand.

Nick pointed, and the path was selected. Paul slowed and allowed Jason to catch up to him from the back of the line.

"Hey," Paul said. "This must be hard for you."

Jason nodded and kept walking, not wanting to talk about it. Paul considered pressing him but decided to change the subject. "I have a question for you, and it may sound strange. Do you remember a time when you were supposed to meet me in our secret spot out in the forest to shoot your brother's BB gun, but you never showed up?"

Jason actually gave a light laugh. "Now that you mention it, I do. Oh man, Michael caught me with it and threatened to beat me up if I didn't do a bunch of chores for him. I felt so bad for not showing, but that was when you caught that horrible flu or whatever and were down and out for like a week."

Paul had no idea what he was talking about but went along with it. To hear that his dream might have some semblance of reality blew him away. If that part was true, what about the other part… with the shadow? Suddenly, the smell of rotting apples, wet leaves, and dirt rushed him, and he bent over, puking up dinner. Jason stopped beside him, setting his hand on Paul's back while he vomited like a frat boy on pledge night. His throat burned by the end of it, and he slumped away from the mess to lean against a tree.

"What was that all about?" Chuck was beside him, and Paul felt like he was going to pass out.

"I… I don't know. Must have been dinner," he lied. It was more than that. The dream, the nosebleeds, the path where he'd woken up… Red Creek was out to get him. Something was buried inside him, and he wasn't sure he wanted to dig it up.

Tyler passed him a water bottle, which Paul graciously accepted and guzzled half of, before rinsing his mouth out and spitting onto the ground. Without thinking, he tried to pass the half-empty bottle back to Tyler, who raised his hands in a "keep it" gesture.

"If everyone is alive, maybe we can keep going. We have a ways to go," Darrel said, urging them on.

Paul was still light-headed, and his throat ached, but he didn't think he was going to pass out any longer, so he stood straight and followed the pack. He wished he had a piece of gum to get the sour taste out of his mouth.

"What was that all about?" Jason asked him, as once again the two of them brought up the rear.

"I don't know. Like I said, something I ate."

"What are you hiding? Do you know something you're not telling me?" Jason's voice grew in volume.

"No, nothing like that. I'm having a hard time being back in the Creek, I guess. Like there's a dam of unwanted memories trying to break out. That's the only way I can really explain it." Paul drank the rest of the bottle, his unsettled stomach happy for the sustenance.

They kept walking, the guys ahead making small talk and tossing out the odd joke Paul couldn't hear, and eventually, they crossed the mile of trees and neared the large barn in the property's corner. This was as far from the main house as you could get, away from watchful eyes.

There was a large secondary wooden fence around the area, which was easy enough to clamber over.

"Shhhh," Darrel said, holding his finger to his mouth in an exaggerated gesture.

Everyone fell silent, listening for any sounds out of the ordinary, but all they got was a steady stream of chirping insects, and the odd hum of a truck on the highway a couple of miles away. Paul strained his ears, thinking he caught a small sound coming from near the barn, but it passed. Probably a mouse or some other rodent scurrying around. There would be a lot of those out here.

"Let's go," Nick said, bravado in his voice.

They made for the large barn doors, and Tyler and Nick circled around the structure, each starting out in opposite directions. A minute later, they were back.

"Nothing to see. Looks like an unused barn." Tyler's flashlight turned off. He hit it on his hand, kicking the battery back in place, and the light came back.

"Time to go in," Darrel whispered, reaching for the

rusty hasp with an old padlock locked around it.

"There's a man door to the side. Let's use that. Less noise," Jason suggested.

Darrel nodded and took out the bolt cutters once again, an invaluable tool for the common criminal.

With a grunt and a snap, the lock fell off the door, and Darrel pushed the wooden slab in with his boot toe. It groaned softly as the unused hinges protested the invasion. Darrel stepped in first, followed by Nick, then Tyler and Chuck. Darrel held the rifle like he was on a SWAT mission, ready to blast someone into their grave. Jason held up a baseball bat, ready to smack a few skulls. Paul held nothing but the flashlight, doubting they would find anything but cobwebs and old hay.

Paul entered the barn and was hit with the smell of decay: moist rotting wood, combined with wet hay. If his stomach had anything in it, he might have thrown up again. The others were spreading out. Paul tried to get his bearings and saw a wall with old tools to the left of him. They looked like they could be a hundred years old and probably were, since the orchard had been there for at least that long. He shone the light, seeing rust caked on them. The roof clearly leaked and had for years.

On the right side was a tractor, and one of the guys was messing around near it, checking the cab for signs of anything. Paul wasn't sure what they expected to find. Tommy wasn't in the barn. He was most likely dead, buried in a field miles away by some country redneck freak with a penchant for taking children. Jason was in and out of horse stables, using a pitchfork to move hay around, in case something was hidden underneath. Paul saw some stairs leading to a loft. Taking care not to step on anything dangerous, he crossed the barn floor. As he neared the stairs, the ground felt different; his steps thudded instead of thumping on dirt.

"Darrel, I think there's something under here," he said, loud enough for his brother-in-law to hear. He stomped on the ground and some dirt flew up, exposing a wooden floor. If he was a betting man, there was a trap door under there. Nick spotted a broom and brought it over. Paul and Darrel moved out of the way while Nick went to town on the dirt. As soon as the dust settled, a wooden door was staring them in the eyes. It had a hand-held metal ring; the piano hinges looked caked with dirt, and Paul wondered if they would even be able to move it.

"This is it," Jason said, staring at it like a man possessed. Paul stepped back as Nick and Darrel grunted and cursed at the heavy door. It didn't budge at first, but soon, it began to lift. Seeing it start to move, they seemed to get more energy, and before they knew it, the trap door was open, flopped over to the other side, leaving a three-by-five-foot opening.

"Who's going down?" Tyler asked, and Paul thought he was going to say "dibs out." Tyler gripped a crowbar and looked ready to use it.

"I'll go," Jason said, shining his light down the set of old stairs that led into nothing but darkness. At once, all six flashlights went out.

"What the hell?" Nick yelled as they all frantically worked to get their lights back on. One by one, the LED lights flicked back to power, except Jason's, which stayed totally dark.

"Guys, that can't be a good sign." Chuck was a pale shade of white. Paul was sure he didn't look any better.

"That was ominous as shit. Jason, you sure you want to do this?" Nick asked.

"What do you guys think is happening here? Are we being haunted by a goddamn ghost? I don't think so. Give me your flashlight, Chuck." Jason stuck his hand out, and Chuck hesitantly passed it over.

Jason started down the stairs, shaking his head. Darrel pushed Paul out of the way and went right behind him, rifle still up, ready for action.

"What do you see?" Nick yelled from above as all four of them stared down the opening, not seeing much past the stairs. The opening must take them deep under the barn. What could this have possibly been used for? A turn-of-the-century storm cellar?

No one answered his question, though they could hear feet shuffling down there still.

"Tell us what's happening, Darrel," Chuck yelled, his voice cracking. Paul was covered in a cold sweat, feeling something familiar hit him. Not from here, but something...

A bang from below caused them to jump, and Paul's heart leaped into his throat.

"I'm going down," Paul said, grabbing the crowbar from Tyler's firm grip. He ran down the stairs, flashlight jostling in one hand, the cold metal of the bar in his right palm. He could hardly hear anything other than the heavy thumping of his heartbeat. Scanning the room, he saw no one.

"Darrel? Jason?" The calls went unanswered. The room was more of a foyer than anything; a bench sat at the foot of the steps, and a closed door greeted him ten feet away. They must have gone through there. With grim resolve, Paul forced his legs to move, stepping across the way before sticking his ear near the door to see if he could hear anything.

When he pulled the wooden slab, it creaked loud enough to send cold through his veins. "Guys, I don't see them yet, but I found a door, and I'm going in!" he called back to the waiting men up top. He heard a muffled response and kept moving. He was in a dirt hallway, cut out of the old ground. It looked like a substantial tunnel, leading God knew where. His feet moved faster as he jogged, looking for a sign of his cohorts. As he ran, his flashlight cut in and out, which he attributed to a jarring battery. By the time he came to a set of doors on the left and right, the hall ended and his light cut out for good.

With a few bashes on the wall, and more than a few colorful swear words, he gave up, jamming the flashlight into his back pocket. The crowbar felt heavier in his hand.

"Darrel. Jason." A muted response made it through the left door, and Paul went that way, ready for anything, or so he thought. He could make out three forms in the dark room: one on the ground, and two standing up. He wanted to rush in, to hit the third man, but he couldn't tell who was who in the blackness.

A gunshot rang loud, the flash lighting the space for a moment, and Paul could only see two men, one now screaming. A flashlight turned on from near the door, shining toward them, and now he could see the picture. Darrel stood, gun raised, over Jason, who was holding his shoulder, blood running between his gripping fingers. The light flickered, and Paul saw something on the wall behind them: a long shadow. Paul bent, grabbing the light, and it came on, full power. The shadow dissipated. Jason was staring at him, mouth open.

"What the hell is going on down here?" Paul yelled.

"I... I saw something... I thought..." Darrel stopped, dropping the rifle before sliding down, back against the dirt wall.

"This crazy brother of yours shot me!"

Paul went over to him, the hair on his neck still raised from seeing the shadow man.

They took off Jason's jacket, which caused him to yell a few times, and saw the bleeding flesh near his bicep. Ripping a piece of his shirt off, Paul wrapped it around the wound, keeping it tight and hoping that it was enough to keep his friend from bleeding out.

"We need to get you out and to the hospital," Paul said. "Darrel, get it together. We need to go!"

His brother-in-law finally seemed to snap to, and stood, helping Paul get Jason to his feet.

They were almost out the door when Jason saw it in the corner, tucked under a sheet of burlap. It was a child's bicycle.

Ten

"*A*nd you're telling me, you guys were out in the forest, drinking beers, and you got shot? Is that correct, Mr. Benning?" Sheriff Cliff couldn't believe these guys. He knew he should be isolating them, making sure their stories checked up against each other and all that, but frankly, he didn't have time or the patience to put up with it at three in the morning.

Benning was wearing a sling, his shoulder bandaged up where the .22 went into his flesh and out the other side. He'd been lucky there. "That's right, Cliff."

"Call me Sheriff Brown, son," Cliff said, knowing no one ever called him that, but at that moment, he'd had enough of the goddamned town. Red Creek could burn in the depths of hell for all he cared. The O'Brians were calling the office every damned hour, asking for updates, and when they weren't calling, they were marching down to his office to ask. If that wasn't enough, they started coming to his house. He got it, they were upset. Hell, if he had any rugrats of his own, he'd probably be pissed too, but right then, he longed for nothing more than to pack up his ten-year-old minivan, peel Ethel away from her soap operas, and get out of Dodge. Maybe head for the west coast. Take their time on the drive, see Yosemite. He'd always wanted to see Yosemite.

"Yes, sir. We were just messing around, shooting cans.

Guess we took it too far." Darrel seemed to be the group's *de facto* leader, but Cliff was more curious about the new-comer hanging out with these guys. He guessed they'd been friends back in the day.

Cliff couldn't believe that the Alenn kid grew up and was in the same room with him now. His head ached, and the coffee only made it worse. Sheriff's office coffee in the middle of the night was now his nightmare. He should have asked Chuck to bring some fresh-brewed with him, maybe threatened jail if he didn't.

Cliff wasn't buying their pitch, but he wasn't going to trudge in the middle of the woods, looking for a can they may or may not have shot at before stupidly shooting each other.

"I take it you're not going to press charges?" he asked Benning, keeping his back to Darrel.

Jason shook his head. "It was my fault for goofing around."

"Fine, get the hell out of here," he said, wondering if he should even bother going home to bed. God knew the O'Brians would be banging on his door in two hours anyway.

The boys started to shuffle out one at a time, but the Alenn kid lingered back. He had to stop calling everyone *kid*. This one had to be closer to forty than thirty, and gray streaked the sides of his hair.

"Who's Sheriff Oliver?" Paul asked him, a serious look on his face.

This took Cliff a little by surprise. He'd been thinking about Oliver the past few days, since the man before him showed up. "Why do you ask?"

"It was a name my mother mentioned in a lucid state, before she forgot who I was and stared out the window."

Cliff had to tread carefully. It was a major cover-up,

one an idealistic young man should have fought. He had a feeling he'd be six feet under if he had, and the new job title hadn't hurt.

"He was the sheriff before me. Oliver Reilly. You probably remember him. Tall guy, thick like a football player gone to fat. Handlebar mustache." Cliff noticed Paul's eyes widening a bit, like he was finally picturing the man he was asking after.

"Thanks. She was probably mumbling. Have a good night, Sheriff Brown. Or morning," Paul said, looking at his watch.

The Alenn kid walked out of the office, but Cliff had a feeling this wasn't quite over. It had been buried for twenty years, but he could smell the freshly dug dirt in the air.

***

*P*aul got in the door without looking down the street to the path between the fields. That was the name he gave it in his head now: "The Path Between the Fields." He thought it would make a great short story title and decided to try his hand at it when he was done with his novel draft. Speaking of his novel, he was dying to get back to it. He'd had two nights of staying up, but energy thrummed through him, and there was no way he was closing his eyes for a while. He'd seen the shadow again, the same damned one from his college experience. And now that he thought of it, all of those times he'd spotted it over the years, which his brain had quickly disregarded as an overactive imagination, were probably real.

What was it? It hadn't hurt them, but Darrel had seen it. Damn right he did. He'd sloughed it off after shooting Jason, but Paul wouldn't forget that look of fear over his brother-in-law's face as he stood there in the dirt basement, smoke wisping from the rifle's barrel.

But there was more to this story – he could see it in the sheriff's eyes – and he was going to find out.

He locked the doors, something they never did when he was a kid, and saw the light on his phone blinking. He imagined a pile of social media notifications and emails, but he saw a dozen missed calls and a few voicemails.

Scrolling through them, he saw most were from his house, one was from Don, and a couple were from Terri's number. That was odd in itself. Had something happened to Taylor? Terri wasn't the type to call him unless it was an emergency.

He dialed his voicemail, set it to speaker, and started to make a pot of coffee.

Beep. 'Paul, it's Terri. I'm in town and we came to surprise you at the condo, but I guess you're away. So you're finally selling the place? Why didn't you tell me? Taylor says hi.' A muffled noise from the background sounded remotely like his daughter trying to say hi over her mother, who was no doubt covering the phone with her palm. *'Anyway, we're here, so call me, or come home.'*

The words were light and fluffy, but he sensed tenseness to them. Something was wrong. Why else would she show up?

Beep. 'Showing went well. Saw your wife, so that was messed up, but she looked great, and Taylor's sure grown up. I think we may get a couple offers by the end of the week, so cross your toes. Call me.' Don's voice carried through the small kitchen and brought him back to his normal life. It was in New York, not this nightmare in Red Creek. He should pack up and leave. Get his things, drive back, and eat brunch with his family.

Beep. 'Paul, where are you? I heard about a missing kid. That's terrible. My dad had surgery and I think it went well. You can never tell with these doctors. Call me, Paul.'

Beep. 'Dad's doing worse, and we have to stay another night. I was going to come to Red Creek. It would be good for Taylor to see her cousin, and … we miss you, Paul.'

His heart almost popped. They missed him. Not just his daughter, but both of them, meaning his wife still cared. He could have danced around the kitchen with a broom if he wasn't so exhausted. He worried for his father-in-law, though. He was a great man, and an even better father to Terri.

Beep. 'Got an offer, buddy. One six. Couple stipulations, but nothing deal-breaker-worthy. I'll email you the dets. Hope the trip home's good. If you're too busy to call, give me an email or a text.'

That was a great offer. He looked in the fridge for some cream and found some old evaporated milk. Was everything in this place a time warp? He added a splash after smelling it and took a sip. Not terrible. Maybe things were looking up. He would start packing the house up now and get ready to move it in the afternoon.

Beep. 'Paul. Remember the shadows you told me about? The ones you saw before? The ones I think you still see?' Terri's voice wavered, and Paul thought her heard a sniffle between the trembling words. *'Taylor swears she saw it. She wouldn't calm down. I ended up snagging some Dramamine from a supply closet at the hospital. We need you. Call me back!'*

Beep. 'End of messages.'

He froze, ice running through his veins. *You still see.* He hadn't seen them for a while. Or had he? He didn't even recall telling her about them. How did Taylor see anything? It was probably just her imagination. Being in a hospital, with her grandpa sick… that would be a lot for anyone.

It was still dark when he dialed Terri back, sitting in the living room among piles of boxes that were ready to go to Goodwill. The phone rang, and his wife answered it in that cute sleepy voice she had when she woke up and was still half out.

"Terri, it's me," he said.

"Paul… what time is it?"

"After five. Sorry for calling so early, but I just got home and heard your messages. Things have been a little crazy here. Is Taylor okay?"

"She's better now, but she's right beside me in our… your bed. She refused to sleep alone."

"How's your dad?" he asked, not trying to avoid the shadow man his daughter had seen, but guessing it looked that way.

"He's not good. The surgery went well, but they're having major complications now. He might not make it. We're heading there again this morning, but Taylor's going to be scared to go back. Hopefully, being there in the day will help. Paul, can we come out there?"

He thought about it, wanting nothing more than to be with his wife and child, but it might be best to not involve them in Red Creek. It was like a dark stain he didn't want them stepping in. It would follow them the rest of their lives.

"Maybe hold tight for today, and I'll call you later. I'm hoping to get done here, and maybe back to the city tomorrow." He meant this but felt in his bones that he wasn't quite done. His jacket hung on the back of the chair by the door. He fumbled through its pockets and pulled out the pill bottle. Prescribed by Dr. Norman. Another name his mother had thrown at him yesterday.

"Did you hear me, Paul?" Terri asked, snapping him back to reality.

"Uhm, sorry, say again?"

"Don needs your address there for the paperwork courier. It can be there today, he said. He only asked me because he couldn't get hold of you. Neither of us could."

He got to the kitchen table, opening the laptop. After a moment of loading, he clicked the starred link in his web browser. The street view of the house he was currently in popped up. He still hadn't memorized the address, so he thought to pull it off the map. He told the address to Terri and almost closed the computer. Instead, he clicked the arrows, moving the view down the street. The path.

"Thanks, Paul. Call me later. Hopefully, Dad gets better, and you get all done. Maybe we can see each other tomorrow," she said. Paul was distracted.

"Sounds good. Kiss Taylor for me."

"I will."

"Terri…"

"Yes?"

"I love you."

"Paul… I love you too." The phone went dead.

The fuzzy picture of the pathway looked at him. The bike he'd seen lying on the ground was there, the same shadowy image in the distance. The bike. They'd never found Jason's kid's bicycle. This could be his son being taken! Was it possible?

With trembling fingers, he found Jason's number in his phone and dialed.

***

"Y ou think someone broke into the orchard last night?" Cliff asked the beautiful blonde. Twenty years ago, she would have gotten his blood boiling – hell, maybe even ten years ago – but old Cliffy was well beyond those years. She could bat her long eyelashes at him all she wanted, it wasn't going to affect him.

"Yes, walk with me for a while." Katherine Smith pulled her purple trench tightly around her, cinching the waist a bit. It accentuated her curves a little more, as if that was possible, and for a second, Cliff thought perhaps his blood could still boil.

"How long have you worked here?" Cliff asked, not really that interested, but it was better than walking in silence. The leaves were falling off the trees, and the dry fall air caused them to lie crisp, crunching with each step. He was still tired, but the half dozen coffees helped. He pushed back the urge to urinate as they moved on. At his age, it was becoming a frequent occurrence.

"Moved back last year. You know how Grandpa got sick, right?" Even her voice was sexy. Cliff shook his head and took a deep breath of brisk morning air.

"Yeah. Cancer, hey? How's he doing?" The old bastard was someone Cliff hadn't wanted to mess with, but unless he wanted his dirty laundry tossed out of the drycleaners, he would play nice.

"He's doing fine." She smiled, but Cliff got the sense she wasn't letting the truth come out. Good. Maybe he'd die, and Cliff could be free from the weight.

"Good to hear. How about you? Are you liking Red Creek?"

She paused, and he almost expected her to say no, that it was terrible. Kids going missing. Rednecks abounding, probably catcalling her every time she went into town. "It's lovely. I have my own guest house with its own pond. And all the apples I can ask for," she said with a giggle.

Cliff smiled through the bullshit conversation. His feet ached, his head hurt, and he was sure the old ulcer was coming back. And now he really had to piss.

"It's up here." She pointed up to the fence line, and in a minute, Cliff could see the cut-out wiring.

"Probably kids. Anything damaged other than this?"

She frowned. "Look, *Sheriff.*" She added a little something to the last word, leaving no mistake on her meaning. "Yesterday, we said no to your little search party, and last night, someone was here. It wasn't *kids.*" She said "kids" with such disdain, Cliff stepped back. She didn't look so alluring anymore.

"Listen to me." He found his backbone and stood up as straight as he could. "I know nothing about this. If someone broke in here and trespassed, then we will file a report. Don't you dare come to me accusing my department of anything." His finger waggled in front of her, and he pulled it back, worried for a second that she might bite it off. Her eyes blazed hot.

"Oh, I know all about the Red Creek Sheriff's Department's integrity. Investigate this, please. I think we might need to get some dogs for the place." She turned, leaving him standing there. What a bitch.

It seemed that the old man passed on the little tidbit about the department to his little granddaughter. For the tenth time that morning, Cliff cursed his old boss.

As he was about to hightail it and return to his car, he saw the snag of cloth on the fence. Blue plaid. He pictured the guys at the station that morning, and one of them had been wearing a blue jacket. He was sure of it.

Eleven

*T*he truck engine shut off, and Paul watched as Jason and Darrel got out and strode up to the house. Jason looked angry, probably a combination of being shot and Paul's cryptic message.

He opened the door, and they entered with solemn greetings. Cool air from outside blew in, giving him some reprieve from the stuffy house. He decided to leave the front door open and lift the screen door window to keep some air flow.

"You guys want a cup of coffee?"

"Show us what you have to show us. My work is already pissed I'm not there today," Darrel said.

"At least you can go tomorrow. How the hell am I going to finish my paving job with a hole in my shoulder?" Jason muttered.

"Look, I said I'm sorry. I thought something was down there with us! I was trying to protect you!"

Paul got between the two men, whose posturing looked like it might end up coming to blows.

"And you were going to shoot a shadow? You really are an idiot, Darrel," Jason said, stepping back and heading for the kitchen. After a moment, he'd calmed, because he came back with a cup of black coffee in his left hand and passed it to Darrel, who smiled at him.

"Thanks."

"Now, Paul. What did you call us over here for? I should be at home trying to sleep so we can go back out there tonight," Jason said.

They wanted to go back to the orchard? That was absurd. Paul had seen the shadow too, and now that someone else had, he knew it had to be real. His mind had thought he was going crazy over the years, but finally, he was validated. It made him think of Taylor, who was only a little girl, and had seen the thing as well. Or things. He didn't know.

"Jason, I know you lost Isaac last year." He stopped and made sure Jason wasn't going to flip out at him mentioning his son. "I looked this place up on street view last week, before I came, and..." He flipped the screen up, and Jason went white.

He grabbed the computer and stared at it from inches away. "Son of a bitch. Son of a *bitch*!"

Paul grabbed the laptop before Jason threw it and broke the thing.

"That's his bike! I know it. We added that blue tape around the handles so he would always know which one was his." Jason was almost vibrating. "Wait, what's that?" He was pointing down the path, where the fuzzy figure looked like he was carrying something, or someone.

"I think it might be Isaac," Paul said, no more than a whisper. The room went deadly quiet, and all he could hear was Jason's ragged breath.

"How could this be? They caught it on film? I remember those weird vans driving around town that day, but no one thought to ask them for the images. Why not? How incompetent are these cops? I'm going to kill Cliff." Jason was still staring at the blurry image, transfixed by it. "We have to go out there and look."

Darrel set his coffee down. "Look. It's been a year.

What good is looking going to do now? You know we searched every damn inch of that area when he was missing. And I know for a fact you were out there every day for three months."

"But we know he was there now. Maybe we can find something else." Jason ran his fingers through his dark hair and kept pacing.

"One more thing. Whose bike did we find last night...you know, down in the barn?" Paul asked.

"It's in my truck," Darrel said. "Let's go have a look."

Paul could tell Jason had already looked and knew it wasn't Isaac's. The bike was insignificant to him now. He lingered back, staring at the computer while Darrel followed Paul outside.

Clouds had come in, and Paul felt light drops falling from the overcast sky. It was going to be a cold rainy day, the kind of day Paul enjoyed back at home. He'd hit a coffee shop, grab a bagel, and work on his latest manuscript while sitting at the kitchen island with the fireplace roaring in the next room. Today wasn't going to be like that.

The bike was covered by a dusty brown tarp that Darrel flung to the side. Under it was a Yamaguchi 2000, red-framed, with scratched handlebars and a decal on the seat.

The world spun around him, and he reached for the truck's tailgate, fingers slipping as he fell down to the road.

"Paul! Paul, what the hell?" He heard the words, but they sounded far away. He looked up, and everything was fuzzy. He must have hit his head.

"Jason! I need your help!" He also heard that and wanted to tell his brother-in-law he was okay. Everything was fine. Then everything went black.

***

Red Creek

*T*he room was musty, reminding him of his grandparents' cellar, where they kept old jars of food no one was ever going to eat. For a moment, he thought he was there, hiding from Beth, maybe; hide and seek was her favorite when she was little. But it had been a year or two since they'd played, Beth saying she was a big girl and didn't play little kid games anymore.

He tried to recall what had happened. Maybe he fell on his bike, and a farmer brought him home. No. That didn't feel right. He felt his head, and there was a bump the size of a small egg growing on it. He brought his fingers back, half-expecting to see blood, but it was dry. Only a bump, then. Good.

There was a lantern hanging on the side of the room, and Paul finally started to panic. He'd never been in real danger before, but this was all wrong. Where was he? The walls were dirt, the ground too. He was underground! A wooden beam straddled the ceiling, supporting the dirt above.

Then it flashed to him. He'd been waiting for Jason to shoot BB guns, and… it had come. The shadow man.

He lunged across the room, grabbing the lantern off its hook, and held it out in front of him. He'd seen someone use one as a weapon in a movie he wasn't supposed to watch. The woman had swung it, hitting the intruder, covering him in flames.

No one came. He paced the small space for at least an hour before settling into the corner of the room. He'd thought about yelling but didn't think the shadow man would be too interested in his cries for release. He'd also seen that never worked in the movies, and he was absolutely sure it wasn't going to work now.

The lantern was dimming, the oil running low. Dried tears crusted to his cheeks. He was too old to cry for his mommy, but he wanted nothing more than to be in her arms right then. He'd give anything.

Hours passed. Days, maybe. His eyelids were heavy on his face, pulling down every chance they got. The lantern flickered softly and *dimmed as his eyes closed, a tired boy drifting to a fretful sleep.*

***

"*P*aul!"

His name snapped him out of the dark and into reality. He opened his eyes, feeling a bump on his head. It was in the same spot as the one in his vivid dream.

"Are you okay?" Darrel asked. His brother-in-law was crouched down over him, eyes frantic and worried.

Paul sat up, head still swimming, and was surprised to find he didn't feel as bad as he'd expected. "I'll be okay." The memory, or dream, or whatever it'd been lingered in his mind. "Guys. That's *my bike.*"

Jason looked at him like he was nuts, head sideways, like a dog trying to decipher if he was getting a treat or not. "What do you mean? How could it be your bike?" he asked before taking a good look at the old BMX. His eyes widened as recognition fired in his synapses. "Holy shit, man. It *is* your bike! How did it get there? I remember you getting that bike when you were around thirteen. Shiny and new. You rode it around like it was no big deal, but I knew you loved your old bike, and God knows your parents didn't have much money."

Paul remembered that new bicycle but didn't know why he'd gotten it. He tried to add it all up together into something that made sense. Nosebleeds. The pathway to the forest where he'd been caught in his dream. Waking up down that path the first night in Red Creek. Antipsychotics. Cryptic apology from his mother. The orchard. The barn where Darrel saw the shadow man too. His bicycle was in that room, and he'd passed out at the sight of it, leading him to a memory of being trapped in that very room. His head swam as they stood there, both men star-ing at him like he would have all the answers they were looking for.

"Guys, I think I was taken when I was thirteen. I think I was in that room under the barn. I don't know much more, but I was waiting for you in the forest that day. Someone took me, maybe some *thing*." Saying it made it feel real, like the dreams and strange events happening around him all of a sudden locked into place; a foothold in his life.

"Wouldn't we know about this? How could you have gone missing and no one ever breathed a word about it?" Darrel said. Jason was sitting down on the curb, his head in his hands.

"I have no idea. We need to go talk to Beth, and maybe my mom. I think the sheriff knows something he isn't say-ing. Jason, something has been taking children from Red Creek, and we've finally found a clue," Paul said.

"Granny Smith's Orchard has to know about it. First they decline to let the search party onto their property, then we find your old bicycle in their barn. We didn't search their fields when Isaac went missing either. But the cops made it seem like that was normal, no need to go there since we had no signs of Isaac. You found Tommy's shoe and it was close. Conway Smith was sick when Isaac disap-peared, and his granddaughter told Cliff they did a thor-ough search, finding nothing. Cliff believed them, and so did I at the time. Damn it, I wasn't thinking clearly. Mary was uncontrollable. She wouldn't stop crying and she was pissed at me about it all, blaming me for him running away. He didn't run away! He was my little angel!" Jason was yell-ing now, and tears ran down his face, dripping onto his jeans as he sat, curling up more as he spoke.

"What's the move?" Darrel asked.

"I don't think we go to Cliff with this. I think he's in on it. He knows something about what happened when I was a kid, but maybe he's working with the orchard. You want to know what the move is?" Paul asked. Jason looked up at him, then nodded his head.

Paul slipped out his wallet and pulled a card from it. "I call this Katherine Smith and ask her out on a date. She seemed to have her eye on me at the bar the other night, so I'll play the rich bachelor author card and see if I can get some dirt." The idea of seducing that beautiful woman seemed so preposterous, but he didn't care. If he could figure out what was stealing Red Creek's children, he'd do almost anything. "We need to find out how many kids have gone missing over the years. See when it all started. Where do we get that kind of information here?"

"County records might have that. It's beside the library up by Gilden. I bet between the two of those, we can get all the details we need." Jason was standing, looking like he had a purpose again.

"What are we waiting for? Let's get this bike inside. God help us if someone who's in on it sees the bicycle from their underground cellar in the back of your truck." Paul lifted it out and hurried it inside. After he grabbed his laptop and locked up behind himself, they left in Darrel's truck. Paul's flesh crawled as they passed the trail at the end of the block. He looked to Jason, who was sitting in the back seat, watching the pathway with fury. If they found whoever had taken his son, Paul didn't want to be the one to get between his friend and them.

***

*T*aylor couldn't believe her mom had brought her back to

the hospital. She'd screamed and fought it until she had no voice left, and no energy to fight anymore, and because of that, she was back in the waiting area outside her grandpa's room. He was going to die. Mom told her he was a fighter, that he would do whatever it took to live, but Taylor could see it in the eyes of the nurses and the doctors that came to update them. He didn't have long.

She wanted to call her dad and talk to him about last night. Mom wouldn't let her. She said he had too much going on, and that they were going to see him very soon. Taylor didn't believe her, since she was the one who'd taken them and moved to California. They should have stayed home, then maybe they could all be together, and she never would have seen that shadow monster.

When she closed her eyes, all she saw was the black ominous form. A stretched-out man made of smoke and darkness. Glowing embers for eyes, like something out of that movie her friend Amy had made them watch at a sleepover. She hadn't been able to sleep that night either. Now the movie monster seemed laughable to Taylor.

"Honey, I'm going to go in and talk to the doctor for a minute. Stay here, and don't go anywhere," her mom said when the man in the white jacket finally went into Grandpa's room. They'd been waiting there for hours for him to show up. Mom said it was typical of a doctor to not think about the people waiting for them.

"But I want to come in with you," Taylor whined, hearing the pathetic sound of her own voice and cringing. She needed to be stronger, like Daddy would be.

"Baby, I have to talk to him about grown-up stuff." Taylor didn't know what that meant, but with her mom, everything seemed to be grown-up stuff.

"Okay, but don't be long," Taylor whispered, feeling her hands start to shake as soon as her mom's back was turned to her.

She was alone in the room now, but it was daytime. She told herself the monster couldn't come out in daylight, and he'd only been in that one hallway. Maybe he was stuck there in that room only. Yeah, he couldn't go anywhere, and he probably didn't even exist. Just like Mommy had said. He was a figment of her imagination. But she knew that wasn't true. He was real, and he wanted to eat her.

A woman came and sat down on the other side of the waiting room. The room was open to the hospital, connected to this wing by a bridge, as Taylor thought of it. The lights flickered a little bit, and when she looked back at the woman, she was gone. Taylor closed her eyes tight, the dread and terror of seeing the shadow monster again filling her every breath. She thought she was going to pass out and tried to breathe like her mommy did when she was meditating. *Deep breaths, everything is okay.* She peeked one eye open and the woman was sitting in the chair, just as she had been, reading a magazine.

Taylor felt silly, like a little baby girl who needed to be coddled. With a defiant new attitude, she told herself she was done being afraid, and she actually felt better for it.

Her mom was gone for some time, and Taylor was bored out of her mind. Just as she considered going into the wing and finding Grandpa's room, her mom came out, her face flushed and wet with sadness.

Taylor ran to her, wrapping her arms around her mom, her safety.

"Honey, Grandpa's no longer with us."

Twelve

"*T*hat's six reported abductions by 1922." Paul marked the name and date down on his spreadsheet. They sat in a semi-private room in the library, paper strewn across the oak table. Red Creek had been nothing more than a farmer's field with a creek running through it back then. The county maps showed around a dozen farmhouses littered among the crops and forested area. The land his mom's house now sat on was nothing more than trees and dirt, according to the map.

He took a picture of it with his phone and did the same with the maps of every decade, all the way up to the 1990s, when they'd stopped having hard copies. Then he emailed the electronic versions of the 2000s and 2010s to himself.

The six had been spread over fifty years, and he didn't have utter confidence in their record-keeping back then. That, and some families might not have told the authorities if something happened. They could have assumed an animal was taking the children, or even runaways. Farm life was tough, and a rebellious teen might have bolted from the life in front of them.

Things had changed by the time the map showed the orchard on it. The 1930 map showed a clear cut of a huge piece of land, and the next one had it labelled as "The Smiths' Orchard" in swirling fancy handwriting.

"Here's another one. 1931, the year Red Creek was

named." Jason scrolled through it, and Paul stood behind him, reading the microfiche over Jason's shoulder.

Peter Bellows became the mayor that year. The article said he was a farmer in the lot adjacent to the orchard and was a pillar of the small community. The article also said his daughter went missing that spring, as the trees were being cut down from what would become Granny Smith's Orchard in a couple years. The search came up empty, but they found part of her clothing, bloody and torn, in the water, and the first thing Peter did was name the town after the blood of his daughter in the creek. The hair on Paul's neck rose as he read the story. Red Creek. He felt his nose, thinking it was running, but his hand came back dry.

After that, the incidents were more frequent. A child or two would go missing every five years until the 1970s, when it became every two years. They made a list of missing children, and over the course of the materials available for the area, it was over seventy.

"Seventy kids, and no one has put it all together?" Paul sat there, staring at the spreadsheet. He imagined the list was much longer, but records could have been lost, not filed, or even removed from history.

"This makes no sense, Paul. How could someone be doing this since the 1800s?" Jason asked, looking through the doorway to make sure he wasn't being watched.

"It's not a person." This from Darrel. "I know what I saw down there, and it wasn't a pervert in a trench coat. It was something else entirely. Something out of one of this guy's books. A monster."

Paul raised his hands in supplication. "Please don't pin this on anything to do with me. I've already had a run-in with the redneck twins at the liquor store."

"Don't worry about those idiots. The only thing they win at is the race to the bottom of another bottle," Darrel grunted. "If you ever run into them again, let me know and I'll help you kick their drunk asses." Paul didn't doubt Darrel had seen his fair share of scraps and was happy the guy was starting to come over to his side. They'd been through something together, and Paul had been the one to run down into that creepy cellar. That meant a lot to Darrel, and he'd told Paul as much.

He went to close the laptop but stopped as he saw a familiar name on the list. He'd been so preoccupied earlier that he hadn't noticed. They'd switched off entering names as they found them, and Jason had probably keyed it in. The name stared back at him from the screen: Timothy Caldwell, missing 1957.

"Guys, look." He pointed to the name. "That's my mother's maiden name. I think I remember hearing my grandfather mention it before. Timothy." He tried the name on his tongue, seeing if it registered anything further. They had a little bit of family in the area, but it started with Paul's grandparents, so that was most likely his mother's brother. His uncle. Uncle Timothy. It still meant nothing to him.

"Holy shit. You think he's related to you?" Jason asked. Paul briefly wondered if having lost a relative to whatever was stalking Red Creek made him closer to Jason in his friend's eyes.

"I think so. I have so many questions for my mom, but I doubt she's going to be able to answer them." He looked at his watch, which told him it was already three in the afternoon. The day had sped past them. His eyes felt tired and strained, both from lack of sleep and from staring at the files and fiche all afternoon, not to mention the bump on his head from falling outside the house earlier in the morning.

"I almost forgot." Paul grabbed his phone and carried

it away, not wanting to make the call in front of listening ears. It had been a long time since he'd asked a woman out on a date, and even though it was fake on his side, it still had his stomach twisted in knots. His wife had told him she loved him that morning, and this same day he was going to ask a hot blonde out on a date.

"Say hi to your girlfriend for me. If she knows anything about my missing son, I'm going to burn her orchard to the ground." Jason said the words so dispassionately it scared Paul.

He grimaced and stepped into another room at the library. This one had a teenage girl in it, twirling her hair around a finger, lips smacking a piece of gum while she stared out the window. She had headphones on, so he grabbed Katherine's card and dialed the number, almost hoping it would go to voicemail so he could hang up and find another way onto the property.

"Katherine speaking." Her voice was like honey, especially after spending a day cramped into that small room with those two guys.

"Hi, Katherine. You may not remember me, but I sure remember you. You slipped me your card on the way out of the bar the other night. Left so fast I couldn't find you in the parking lot when I went after you." Paul felt like she was going to see right through his lies.

"Oh, I might recall that. I also may have had a few too many. I'm afraid I'm not normally so forward." Now it was Paul's turn to not believe what she was saying. "I was beginning to think you might never call, Paul."

"Wait, how do you know my name?"

"Your friend… the big oafish one. He told me. I had to buy him a beer first," she said, and Paul pictured Nick drunk as a skunk, making this woman buy him a beer for a name. He almost laughed.

"I see. I've been busy packing up my mom's house, and then with the O'Brian kid going missing. It's been terrible." He fished with the kid, hoping to get a bite.

"I know. We scoured the orchards for any sign of the little guy, but there wasn't a hair to find. I pray each day for his safe return." Her voice dripped with concern, but it was painted on so thick he knew it was just a show. His gut was telling him the Smiths knew something. It would be hard not to, being the center of so much pain for so many years. The maps of the area showed the abductions increasing when their orchard went in. That couldn't be a coincidence.

More likely, though, she was family brought in to deal with the company while her sick grandfather took to his bed. Paul wanted to give her the benefit of the doubt. Anyone from out of town, forced to leave their lives and live in Red Creek, might have a certain level of phony to put on for the simple folks that lived here. A few days ago, Paul would have turned his nose up at them right alongside her, but after everything that had been going on, he felt like one of them.

"So do I. What do you say to dinner out with me tonight? It'll be good for us to take our minds off things for a while." His heart raced, nervous for all the wrong reasons. Or the right ones, maybe.

"It's short notice, but if I move a couple things around, I should be able to. How about we hit Emilio's in Gilden? It's much nicer than the options here in the Creek. Pick me up at seven? I'm on the way," she said with a confidence Paul actually found appealing.

"Sounds like a plan. See you then."

"I look forward to it." The honey-dipped voice lowered as she said this last bit before she hung up. He sat there holding the phone to his ear for a moment before realizing she was off the call. The girl at the table had her headphones off, and she stared at him, chuckling to herself. He blushed for some reason and hightailed out of the room.

"Have a hot date?" Darrel asked, the two of them waiting by the exit.

"Tonight, Emilio's. I'm picking her up."

"We have to go back. I need to see more of that barn," Jason said with a finality Paul didn't like.

"Are you guys crazy? Remember what happened down there?" Paul asked, shaking his head.

"Yeah, your brother-in-law flipped out, seeing some shit that wasn't there. I know you might believe him with this shadow business, but I don't. I think some freak is living out there, taking kids. They're probably passing it down every generation, a family of freaks, all taking our children. We go there, we get more information, and we end this." A vein on Jason's forehead pulsed.

"Beth is going to kill me," Darrel said as they left the library.

"Let me talk to her tonight and see what I can learn. Give me the night, please. If we learn nothing new, I'll try to get another date, and I'll keep her out tomorrow. Then the crew can go in again and scope it out." Paul didn't want them walking into anything without him. He *did* believe in the shadow man. Hell, he'd seen him at least a dozen times since that alley in college, and the apparition had never hurt him. Maybe he wasn't the bad guy. Maybe he was there to help.

"Fine. One day. But only because I'm tired as hell, and I was shot last night." Jason smiled and punched Darrel in the shoulder.

"Shotgun!" Paul called and saw Jason wince at his choice of words. "Too soon?"

The three of them piled into the truck, and for a moment, it felt like a camaraderie he'd been missing out on for years. There was a huge difference between having wine with his friends at a snooty restaurant in the Upper East Side and slapping backs with these guys in Red Creek. It almost felt like he was home.

It was five when they dropped Paul off, once again promising not to go all Scooby Doo gang without him. Beth had called Darrel while they were on the road, and she demanded he get home to be with them. She told him there was to be no more running around with pitchforks at night, and to leave her brother out of their shenanigans. If she found out that she'd been on the truck's speakerphone with other people in the cab, she'd have blown a gasket.

He decided to take a shower before calling Terri to see how her day was. He'd texted her earlier, but she hadn't replied yet. Probably still at the hospital.

Being in the house was still eerie, and he was looking forward to getting the boxes and furniture out of there. Seeing the things that had lined their shelves when he was a kid was hard. They turned to clutter as more stuff accumulated, stayed in the house; nothing was ever disposed of. Why had his mother become like that? Everything going on had disrupted their timeline, but he and Darrel had committed to moving it out tomorrow. Nick and Tyler told Darrel they'd come after their morning shifts at the road crew site, to give a hand. Paul appreciated their efforts. His friends in the city would scratch their heads and recommend three different moving companies, depending on if you wanted speed or lower price.

The bathroom was small. He couldn't believe they'd shared that avocado green bathtub the whole time growing up. The basement was plumbed in for a shower drain when they had a structural issue covered by insurance, and Paul's dad had always promised to add the second bathroom. The furthest he got on with it was adding in a toilet to the unfinished room, a curtain hanging in the doorway for privacy. Paul and Beth had been so excited they could go to the washroom while the other was taking their sweet time in the main bathroom. He smiled as he thought of something so small being such a big deal at that time of their lives.

The light was getting dim through the window, and he flicked on the lamp. The lampshades on the vanity fixture were dark, a layer of dust covering them. He made a mental note to clean them when he was done. He stepped into the shower and onto the rubber grip mat; the tension slipped from his shoulders as the hot water steamed against his back.

A noise came from the outside. The white lace curtains pushed aside, he wiped the now steamed window pane with his left hand, leaving a transparent streak to look through. This time of year, the sun was down earlier every day, and it was already behind the trees in the west, casting a dim shade over Red Creek. The yard was fairly large, a few birch trees lining the sides, with the back up against the canola field. Another clunk from behind the house, perhaps from the other side of the fence. Maybe it was the farmer working on something outside their yard.

Sticking his head under the old-school shower head, Paul tried to push it all away and just be in the moment. The hot water washed away the day's stresses and cleansed his mind and body for the upcoming evening. His scratches had healed to light lines on his face and arms, and he hardly even noticed them anymore.

Another thud emanated from the back yard, the sound carrying through the window with a shake of its glass against the wooden frame. Through the steam, he could make out something moving inside the yard, along the rear fence. His relaxing shower was over; it had turned to *get some clothes on and try to not have a heart attack while seeing what is outside.*

His foot slid on the yellowing linoleum when he stepped out of the tub, and he grabbed for anything as he fell, dragging the shower curtain down on top of him.

A stream of curses coursed out of him as he lay sprawled on the bathroom floor, his legs bent up against the toilet. Getting up gingerly, he checked for injuries, and was sure his head was no worse than it had been from the fall in the morning. Red Creek was out to get him.

By the time Paul got his jeans on, found a hammer as a weapon, and was out the back door, the streetlights were turning on, and the backyard was empty save for a couple of crows looking for a sad meal. The birch trees' leaves had turned a pale yellow, and most of them had left for the year, creating a blanket of auburn over the grass. He used to hate raking leaves in the autumn, and if he wasn't spending the evening shirtless and looking for an intruder, he probably would have laughed at the fact that he'd have to rake it one last time.

No one could have been hiding behind the sparsely covered trees, so he made for the back shed, his bare feet seeming to find every pinecone or rock in the yard.

The hammer was held chest high as Paul made his way to the run-down wooden shed. He could smell the rot as he neared it, a pungent cedar odor once fresh, now reminding him of an old coffin.

"I saw you. Come out and I won't call the cops." He didn't expect someone to come out from inside the shed with their arms raised in the air, but he did think he might be able to hear someone rustling around.

A memory of his dream flashed through his mind: a

shadow looming over him, smoke pouring off its body. He became self-conscious of only wearing pants and felt like eyes were watching him as he reached for the latch. The hasp was loose, meaning someone could be inside. He pushed the bottom corner of the door, and it creaked open. Ready for anything, his heart raced faster than ever, but the shed was empty. Not of things, but no one was inside the five-by-ten space. Beth's bicycle sat on top of his newer one, bought to replace the missing one they'd found last night.

Garden tools lined the back wall, unused in years, he was sure. Various ceramic pots were stacked in the left corner, a corn broom leaning against them. Cobwebs filled all available spaces on the ceiling, and Paul made out a spider or two hiding in the shadows. The shadows. He could still feel eyes on him, and decided it was time to head back in. It was probably only his imagination; the whack on his head earlier was making him see spots that weren't there. Maybe that was the explanation for all the times he'd seen the shadow man. He would go see a doctor when he got back to the city; a CT scan would be able to see if he had a tumor growing on his brain, or maybe it was all mental. A shrink was what he needed.

The city felt like another lifetime ago. Where were the files Don was supposed to courier out? What day did he speak to Terri about them? Was it today? Paul's head throbbed again, and as he was about to shut the wood-slatted door, he saw it. It was still smoldering in the crisp evening air. A handprint, black as midnight, was imprinted on the right wall, near the ceiling. With trepidation, he stepped inside, feeling that whatever made that print was long gone. The rationale made no sense, but he pushed the fear aside for a moment and pushed his own hand out, holding it inches away from the blackened one. His fingers were a good three inches shorter than the imprint's, the smell of burning wet wood filling his nostrils with a memory.

Smell was a funny thing. Something buried deep down could be activated with as little as a scent. He'd read somewhere that smell was more tightly linked to memory than sight. As he stood there, wanting to bottle everything up, he understood this more than ever.

He left in a hurry, leaving the shed door wide open. Inside the house again, he slammed the door shut and locked it. The idea that a lock would stop whatever he was up against made him laugh. He stood there chuckling like a maniac, with his bare back against the cold metal of the back door.

Thirteen

"*P*aul's going out there, and by himself?" Beth could feel her face flush. Her husband could be so stupid. At least he'd had enough common sense to tell her everything, even about him shooting Jason. Dear God, all this shadow talk. It had her remembering that autumn Paul went bonkers, and they had to send him to that doctor. All he would talk about was that shadow, and it had scared Beth half to death. He'd wake up in the middle of the night screaming. They had to keep all his lights on and add more so nothing in his room would cast any more than a tiny gray shadow on his floor. Even those set him off. It only lasted a couple weeks before he was normal again, and Beth had been so young, she'd honestly forgotten until Darrel brought up this thing he'd seen.

"Yeah," he nodded, "but what were we supposed to do? Go on a date with him?" Darrel walked past her, opened the fridge, and grabbed one of his precious beer cans, cracking it before the cold air of the appliance dissipated.

"What the hell is he doing going on a date with that woman?" Paul was still married, and from everything Beth could tell, he was desperately obsessed with his wife.

"He's not doing it to nail her. Not that I'd blame him if he did." Darrel jumped back from her swinging fist. What an ass she'd married. Still, he was trying to help Jason and the others by finding little Tommy. It was more than the sheriff's department seemed to be doing.

"Mommy, I'm hungry," Isabelle said, rubbing a small hand over her stomach. God, Beth loved that little girl. She was the light that kept her going every morning, afternoon, and night.

She stepped over to her daughter, and pulled her close, hugging her in a smothering mother kind of way, and Issy hugged her back for a few seconds before trying to wriggle away.

"Dinner's almost done. Pork chops and veggies." The combination didn't do much for her girl's expression. "And some pie for dessert, if you eat it all." This brought a wide, gap-toothed smile from her baby girl.

Isabelle started to set the table without even being asked, and Beth beamed inwardly. She looked at her husband, standing there shaking his nearly empty beer, and knew which parent Isabelle took after.

A few minutes later, Beth was sitting down with her family, wishing Paul was with them. The clock hit seven as she reached over, grabbing a spoonful of steamed carrots.

***

*I*t would only take ten minutes to get there, so Paul dialed Terri as he got into his car, letting the Bluetooth speakers work for him. It rang once, and she answered it.

"Dad's gone," she said. He could picture her fiddling with her hair, soft cheeks wet with sadness.

"I'm so sorry, honey. I loved that man." He genuinely did. More than his own father, not that they'd had much of a relationship. "How are you doing?"

"I'm a mess, but considering it's just me and Taylor

here, I'm hanging in there. I miss you. Do you think you can get to the city?" He heard the longing in her voice, the need for love from another adult. Someone to share a glass of wine with and talk nice things about her father. It pained him to say he couldn't.

"I'm almost done here." What day was it? It was only Tuesday. It had felt like weeks, but it was only a few days since he'd arrived. "I should be back Thursday." He didn't know if that was true and had a sinking feeling it wasn't going to be. It was close enough for her to not freak out at him, and if he had to push it a day or two after, she probably wouldn't leave before he could get back. Probably.

"I was going to come out there if things got better, but now I have to deal with all the lawyer stuff and plan a funeral. Paul, how am I going to do this?"

"Do what you can, and I'll be there soon enough. Can I talk to Taylor?" He was getting close to the orchard entrance, and his nerves were starting to get to him. Between that and learning about his father-in-law passing away, and seeing the handprint in the shed, he thought he might be losing his mind. The pill bottle he'd found still sat in his jacket, and he pulled them out, pushing them into the console compartment.

"She's sleeping. She misses this place. Her old room."

"It misses her too."

"Maybe… did you get the papers from Don?"

"No. They didn't show up. I'll call him later and double-check he sent them to the right address."

"You don't have to sell, you know."

Paul pulled over to the side of the gravel road, the dusk light dim, as the stars began to shine down from above. "I don't need that much room."

"We could… I left my place in LA. Threw our things in storage." She was leaving words out, and he knew she was implying something he'd wished for so many times. Now he was worried she was doing it for the wrong reasons.

"We can talk about it later this week. Tell Taylor I love her. Have a good night, T. I'm so sorry about Dad."

"Thanks. Text me later. I want to know you're safe. I can tell you're out driving. I have a feeling tonight." Paul's stomach flopped. So did he.

"I will. Love you."

"Love you too."

The call ended, and he looked up to the looming gates at Granny Smith's Orchard: black cast iron across the gravel. The name was ornately built into the rods, painted in blood red. Paul thought it curious, since Granny Smith apples were green. He'd been there when he was a kid, one time when his dad was doing deliveries for the Smiths. The place had seemed magical then. Bright sunshine, rows upon rows of gorgeous fruit-bearing trees, the house so shiny and huge he'd thought a king and queen must have lived there. His dad had laughed at that, a great booming laugh like Paul had told the funniest joke in the world. Tonight, the house rose in the distance, dark in the sliver of moonlight's touch.

The clock shone seven-o-nine and he cursed himself for being melodramatic. Sometimes a house was a house, and a shadow was just that. A shadow.

He drove up to the gate, where a speaker sat on a pole in the ground. Window rolled down, he hit the buzzer and heard it ring quietly.

"Hello," a tinny voice called to him.

"I'm here to see Katherine. My name's Paul Alenn."

The gate buzzed and slid almost silently to the left, letting him drive past into the orchard grounds. It was around two hundred yards to the mansion beyond. To the side of it was their storefront, where you could buy anything apple-related. Candy apples, apple pie, apple crumble, apple wine. He and Jason had snuck a bottle of that sweet wine from Jason's mom's wine rack one hot summer night. After one drink, Jason had Paul convinced he should go knock on Chrissy's window and invite her out. She joined them, after a minute of saying they had something really cool to see. He'd kissed her for the first time that night, the taste of apples lingering on their lips.

God, what was he doing? About to go on a date with someone other than his wife and dreaming about his first kiss with another girl. He needed to get out of this town.

He considered backing up and leaving, claiming he was sick, and got so far as to shift into reverse when the gate slid shut behind him. With resigned determination, he drove up to the house and parked at the start of the round-about, behind a dark Range Rover. Feeling like a teenager picking up his prom date, he got out of his car, taking the long walk up the front walk and onto the sweeping front porch. It even had the swing bench fastened on chains, creaking in the wind.

Before he got to the door, it swung open, soft orange lighting spilled out of the warm house. Katherine stood there, looking every bit as attractive as she had in the bar, but now she had a slinky red dress on, with high heels. He was glad he'd brought the sportcoat.

"Hello, handsome," she said confidently. "Hope you had no trouble finding the place."

"Everyone knows where Granny Smith's is."

"I forget that sometimes. Change of plans. I thought we could stay in and have dinner here." The smell of basil and tomatoes wafted through the house and outside. If he wanted to learn more about the place, this was working in his favor.

"Sure, sounds great. And smells even better." He smiled and entered the house. The first thing he noticed was how understated it was. He'd imagined it would be full of opulence and grandeur, but though it was large and classic, the fixtures and art were more rustic than wealthy and gaudy.

"Come on in." She walked in front of him, and he tried to avoid watching the swaying of her hips in that tight dress. He had to keep his eyes on the prize, and that wasn't her. Her heels echoed off the wooden plank floors leading them from the foyer, through the large open-ceiling living space, a huge stone fireplace roaring and crackling.

"Nice place," he said as they walked into the kitchen. It was large, an island dominating with a copper farmhouse sink. He liked the style. Water boiled in a pot on the gas range, beside a saucepan that was dribbling red sauce off the sides.

"I'd like to take credit, but I've only been here a year."

"Who else lives here?" Paul asked.

"Only my grandfather and his health care worker, Marge. Grandmother died a couple years ago, then he got sick last year. They were looking for someone to come and run the business, and that's where I come in." She smiled; her attempt at a sweet smile, he guessed. It was.

"What about your parents?" he asked.

"My mom never wanted this life. They live in Florida now." She grabbed a bottle of wine from the counter, the cork already off, the tannins airing out. "Wine?"

"Yes, please." Paul took a tall stemmed glass, three-quarters full after her generous pour. He almost took a sip, but he stopped, telling himself to be more cautious. This wasn't real. If he was right, the missing children originated from this orchard's land, and the Smiths were the owners. She raised an eyebrow at him and took a drink of her wine.

This eased his tension, and he clinked her raised glass before tasting the bold red. He was no stranger to fine wines, and this one fit the bill.

"What made you change your mind?" he asked, leaving her looking at him questioningly. "I mean, about going to Emilio's."

"One thing I know is that small towns love their gossip. If the new girl in town was seen on a date with the return of Red Creek's prodigal son, imagine the flapping tongues. Even in Gilden, news travels fast back to the Creek," she said, mischief in her eyes. "So I decided to put my go-to Italian dinner on the menu and figured you wouldn't mind a home-cooked meal."

She must have known he was separated from his wife. If Nick had told her his name for a beer, surely everything he knew about Paul was on the table.

"I wouldn't mind at all. Can I help with anything?" he asked. "Is that garlic bread I smell?" The scent rose from the oven and across the room. He hadn't eaten anything in a long time, if that diner in Gilden had even counted as food this morning, and his stomach growled at the sight of the glorious meal.

"No need to help. Everything should be ready soon."

Paul saw the fresh-made noodles hanging on a rack beside the boiling water. She'd gone all out.

"How do you like Red Creek?" he asked, curious to see how she'd answer a heated question like that.

She shrugged, blue eyes twinkling. "It's not what I expected. I used to visit when I was a kid, and we rarely went into town, so all I knew was this place. The rich house, huge grounds, employees around, and that was Red Creek to me. Then I come here, and I see a run-down town, no industry, no leadership, and no motivation from the people. It was a harsh reality. And when I tried to make friends, they were hard to come by."

The words fit his thoughts on the town to a T. It took coming from the outside to see it, apparently. Instead of agreeing, he nodded along, letting her continue.

"It's been a little lonely, to be honest." She walked closer to Paul, where he sat on a stool at the island. She was close enough to touch him, and she set her left hand on his knee. Before he could panic, the water on the stove boiled over, causing her to rush over and turn it down. "Well, that's the water telling me it's ready for the pasta." She smiled over her shoulder and went to work.

Maybe staying in hadn't been the best of ideas. He took another sip of wine. It was time for some reconnaissance work. "Where's the bathroom? I'd like to wash up."

She pointed to the far side of the living room. "Past the fireplace, down the hall. Second door on the left." She was busy lowering the fresh noodles into the angry water, and he slipped from the room. He thanked her and crossed the space, feeling eyes on him. He turned back; Katherine was focused on her cooking. Scanning the walls, he saw paintings, but none with the moving eyes he expected from a cartoon, not real life.

The bathroom door was open, but he kept walking down the hall. Flickering lights came from a mostly shut door on the right. That would be the master bedroom of this floor. More than likely, there was a whole wing of bedrooms upstairs, but for a sick old man, he would be on the most accessible level.

Paul crept down the hall, trying to keep his noise to a minimum, which was hard on the old creaking floorboards. Back against the wall, he leaned to the side, peering into the partially open door. A television rumbled at low volume as the screen's ambiance made the man in the bed glow. Beside him sat a middle-aged woman in a gray sweater, squinting as she read a tattered old paperback novel. The man's eyes were open; deep purple bags hung like overripe fruit. The blankets were pulled up to his chest, but there was no mistaking that the old man was sick and wasting away. If Paul was working at a carnival "guess-your-weight" station, he'd peg the guy at about one-twenty.

Katherine called to him from the kitchen, and he quickly moved his head away from the door, but not before catching something moving from the corner of the room. His heart pounded, wondering if they'd seen him, and if that was the shadow man or a result of the flickering television. Sweating now, he stepped away and quickly entered the bathroom, where he locked the door and sat down on the toilet seat lid. Watching under the door, he had the feeling it was going to slip underneath, like a monster from an old *X-Files* episode, but nothing appeared.

"It was just the TV, and they didn't see you peeking in, or they would have said something," he told himself. He knew he'd better get out of the washroom before Katherine thought he was in there leaving his mark on the place.

He flushed the unused toilet and washed his hands, splashing some cold water on his face.

The towels were soft; an old towel that was bought with care and concern. The towel couldn't distract him from the anxiety that was crawling up from his feet, though. What was he doing there? Terri needed him. The mystery surrounding Red Creek was getting bigger each day, and Paul felt himself caught in the middle of it. An ancient evil embedded in the land. The writer in him took the story and rolled with it. This story didn't have a happy ending, of that he was sure.

As he was reaching for the door handle, a soft knock echoed, a jostle of the knob.

"Paul? Are you okay?" It was Katherine.

Unlocking it, he opened the door, and smiled wide.

"Sorry, had a phone call I had to take. I apologize for leaving you for so long." It had only been a couple minutes, and she had tried to come into the bathroom. That was strange, but what about the week hadn't been? "My realtor is selling my townhouse, and the paperwork he sent didn't make it today. He was royally miffed with the courier and wanted to assure me it was coming tomorrow."

She looked to buy the story. "Dinner's ready. I'm going to check on Grandfather and let Marge know I'll leave her some leftovers. Be right there."

She swayed down the hall, heels echoing off the floor once again. Paul, heart still pumping, went back to the kitchen, wishing the fire was a little lower as his core temperature rose.

Katherine came back, face with a little less color than it had before.

"Everything okay?" he asked.

She nodded and tried to smile, but it quickly disintegrated into a sob. Tears streamed down her face, and Paul stepped in, embracing her while she cried on his shoulder. It felt so odd to hold another woman. Human contact had been so far from his daily routine over the last two years that now it felt alien. His hand was around her waist, and when she seemed to let up a bit after a minute, he tried to slowly pull away, which brought her arms tight around him. Her face pressed in the nook of his neck, which was now wet, and she didn't move it for a few moments.

He'd always been a sucker for a damsel in distress. It had been his downfall more than once in college, and he'd thought he was past it. She finally raised her head, looking him in the eyes. He wanted nothing more than to push her back and get out of there before he did something he'd regret. To hell with the old man, the shadows that danced out from his damaged mind, and the wife that left him high and dry two years ago, taking his precious daughter with her. As he looked at Katherine's gorgeous silver-blue eyes, he felt the urge to press his lips to hers, to taste her lipstick, and slide that slinky dress to the floor.

It must have been a full minute with no one speaking, them playing a game of cat and mouse, before he came to his senses and stepped back, clearing his throat. Katherine blushed, and looked genuinely embarrassed.

"I remember you," she said softly.

The words chilled his hot blood.

"It was a long time ago, and I was about to head back home from a summer here with my grandparents. I saw you with the police. You were a couple years older than me, brown unruly hair. You looked like you'd been through something terrible, but those eyes. They were haunted and wonderful at the same time." She took a sip of her wine. "They still are."

"Where was this?" he asked, hands shaking.

"Outside the orchard. We drove by, and I asked Grandma to stop, but she wouldn't. She looked really mad. I asked her about it, but she ignored me, and when we got back, she and Grandfather went outside and argued for a good hour. I snuck away and ran to the gate, but you were gone already."

"How do you know it was me?"

"I asked around before I left. Paul Alenn, they told me. You were the only boy that matched my description. I was just a little girl, hopelessly infatuated with a troubled boy I'd only glimpsed. When I saw you the other night at the bar, I thought there could be no way. Over twenty years, and I could still pick you out of a crowd."

"And you never found out what I was doing, or why I was with the police? Was there anyone else with us?" He asked the questions in a barrage, standing tall and intimidating. He could see the worry in her face, and he forced himself to calm down. The wine slid down his throat in one large swallow. "I'm sorry. I don't remember anything about that."

She looked uneasy. "What do you mean? You'd think a kid would remember a run-in with the cops."

He shook his head, sitting back down on the stool. "Nothing. I think I repressed it." He stopped himself, not wanting to get into it too deeply with a Smith. He was sure they were involved with it all. He didn't get that sense from Katherine, but she might be acting along, like the helpless little girl looking for a strong man to be her rock. This woman was anything but, and he knew it the instant he laid eyes on her.

"I'm sure it was nothing." He tried to wave it off like it was no big deal, but her seeing him back then made it all too real. Before, he could have said it was only made-up dreams. The bike could have been stolen, and ended up in the orchard barn, by a kid who broke in there, but now... now he knew it all to be true. "Is your grandfather... okay?"

She shook her head. "It's spread throughout. He won't be with us long." Her eyes brimmed with tears again, but Paul wasn't going to get brought into her arms again. If he was, he wasn't sure he'd escape. Or want to.

"How about some more wine?" He poured them another glass and went to the stove to see if he could salvage the overcooked pasta. The sauce was still simmering lightly and smelled wonderful. Katherine watched him as quiet music played through ceiling speakers, Bach's "Toccata and Fugue" came on, and Paul almost laughed at the ominous song's implications for his week. Katherine didn't seem to notice it, and soon they were sitting at the romantically decorated table, eating what Paul guessed was even tastier than whatever Emilio was serving that night.

They chatted long into the evening about life, what they liked to read; she asked about his life as a writer, and he told her about his fear of failure and how pumped up he was about his new project. He realized he'd gone a few days without writing, and he missed it greatly. It had become such a big part of him, but his new book would have to wait until Red Creek played out. He had the feeling a bigger idea was going to blossom from the mess he found himself in.

He was getting a little drunk and felt it when he stood to use the bathroom at about ten. Katherine laughed lightly as he stumbled, claiming his foot was asleep. The wood fire was all but glowing embers at that point when he passed it. The light at the hall's end was gone. Marge would have gone to bed, Katherine said; her grandfather had zonked out long ago.

The light didn't turn on as he hit the switch. He fumbled with it a few times, rocking it on and off, but nothing happened. His head was swimming, and he tried to recall who had poured the last glass of wine. Had it been him or her? It was her! He turned, grasping at the wall, and held himself up. Goddamn him for thinking this had been a good idea. He took small determined steps back toward the kitchen. The lights were out there too, the front door wide open.

"Katherine!" he called groggily, but no answer came.

A loud bang sounded from outside. Had that been a gunshot? His legs were going to give out, and he could feel the drug numbing his body as well as his mind. "Katherine, you bitch!" he tried to call out, but some guttural animal noise escaped his clenched teeth instead. In the darkness, he thought he saw a shadow emerge, crossing the room in a slow glide. His eyelids were too heavy to keep open, and in a final slump, he fell in a heap on the wooden planked floor.

Fourteen

"*W*e're going to have to stop meeting like this," Cliff said through the BMW's open window. Paul Alenn was slumped in the driver's seat of the car that was down in the leaf-covered ditch. The back roads were dangerous this time of year, animals running across the roads at dusk and dawn, causing more than a few accidents, but the car didn't look damaged from his vantage point.

Paul's eyes slowly opened; red lines were deep in their pale whites. He looked like shit. Cliff leaned in and smelled a thick waft of booze emanating from the car. So that's how it was.

"Sheriff..." Paul looked around at his situation, as if trying to recollect where he was and what he'd been doing. "She did this! We have to go arrest her!"

Cliff almost guffawed at this. "She? Who is *she*?"

"Katherine Smith."

"It just so happens she's the one who called us, Mr. Alenn. She told Gloria you went out there last night, drunk as a skunk and acting very shady ..." Cliff looked for a reaction. He got one.

"What? No way. I went over there... looking for something, and she made me dinner, drugged my wine... I passed out, now here we are." Paul's voice was up an octave, his words pouring out so fast Cliff had to let his brain catch up.

"Look, I still need to bring you in. You smell like a wino, you're in the ditch, and we have a case of breaking and entering to deal with. Not to mention this is the second time I've found you passed out in the wilderness in a few days." Cliff opened the door, and Paul came pouring out.

He decided cuffing the guy wasn't necessary. Hell, he was starting to believe Paul's story. Those damned Smiths were up to something, and maybe Paul could help him find out what. The world's most unlikely duo. They passed the car's back seat, and a jacket caught Cliff's eye. It was blue plaid. Bingo.

"Is that yours, son?"

When he thought Paul couldn't look any more dejected, he managed it then.

***

*T*he pieces of the puzzle were all around him, surrounding him in the dark cloud of Red Creek. Unfortunately, he only knew where half of them were, and they didn't make anything remotely close to a clear picture. His cell was sterile, probably mostly unused since it was built, with the exception of the odd drunk tank or wife beater, if he was to guess. He was neither of those, though he probably looked like a mix of the two at that moment.

Wednesday morning. Hump day. The stupid thought made him laugh, like only a madman in a cell alone could do.

A door clicked open down the hall, and a weary Sheriff Cliff walked over to the edge of the bars. Pulling a key ring from his belt, he unlocked the doors, looking Paul in the eyes the whole time. It was a little unsettling. "Come with me, son," he said.

Paul followed him on stiff legs. He felt like crap. One of these days, he was going to need a night's sleep. If he made it out of this station, he was going to make straight for home. He was officially done with Red Creek. He would leave them all behind to let their kids be stolen by the orchard monster or Grandpa Smith. Either way, both were monsters, of that he was certain.

He was led into a small room with no window, a chair on either side of the old wooden square table, and one more pressed up against the wall in case they needed to good cop/bad cop anyone.

"Have a seat." Cliff pointed across the room, and Paul obliged him.

A woman knocked on the door, bringing in a tray with two cups of coffee and a couple of water bottles.

"Thank you, Gloria," Cliff said, taking the tray. She left without saying a word, but he noticed a quick glare in his direction from the portly woman.

"Paul, a few people have called in, accusing you of some pretty bad stuff." Cliff took a sip of coffee and slid the other across the table, liquid jumping over the edge of the Styrofoam cup, spilling a few blobs on the wood.

Paul's stomach was already hurting, and the idea of coffee in it made him nauseous, but he took the cup and sipped it. "What can they be accusing me of?" he asked.

"First, Katherine Smith claims you were near her house last night, drunk and acting very suspicious. She also had me out there yesterday morning, showing me her cut fence, where someone presumably broke into their orchard. I found this–" Cliff placed a torn piece of cloth on the table "–stuck to the cut fence, and what do you know? It matches the jacket we found in the back of your car. I suppose you're going to tell me she planted that too?"

Paul shook his head solemnly. "I told you what

happened with Katherine last night already, but that's Darrel's jacket. I'd borrowed it."

"To do what?" Cliff asked.

Paul juggled the idea of telling him everything. The shadows, the Smiths, the list of missing kids. He knew about Paul when he was a kid, and that linked him to it all. Unless he was on their side, but even if he was, what did he have to lose? He decided to err on the side of caution.

"We broke in."

"You broke into the orchard? Who is we?"

He had to be careful not to get everyone in trouble, but Cliff wasn't a dumb man. He'd seen the gunshot wound and all of them together.

"I think you know who. Tommy is missing, and everything points in the direction of that orchard."

"How so? Enlighten me," Cliff said, leaning forward a little. This told Paul that Cliff agreed to some extent, like he'd been waiting for someone to tie it together for him. It couldn't be easy having so many missing persons never solved under your watch, and the tired look on Cliff's face painted that picture pretty clearly.

Paul took a deep breath. "Do you remember me? From when I was a kid?"

Cliff's mouth opened a little, like he was about to say something, then closed. It reminded Paul of a fish. When he spoke, his voice had lost any of its intensity. His posture was less firm too, like the air had been let out of his tires. "I do. But I take it you don't."

Paul shook his head. "I'm beginning to see a bit of the picture. Tell me what you recall of it."

All of a sudden, the sheriff was the one being interrogated, but if he noticed, he didn't let on. "It was another one of those cases. You were the second kid to go missing that year, and the town was ready to raise pitchforks and clear our department out. Before that, it had been a couple of years, and we were hoping it was over." Cliff sipped from his cup, looked Paul in the eyes, and took a flask out of his jacket's interior pocket, splashing some brown liquid into his coffee. He reached it out to Paul, who took a splash in his as well.

"You were hoping what was over?" Paul asked, prompting an answer he already knew.

"Red Creek has a history. We've lost over one hundred children over the last century or so."

A hundred? It was a few more than they'd found in the record books.

"Let me guess, Paul. You've done your own research and found it slightly less than that? That's because *they've* buried as many as they could; swept them under the rug. Paid off families." The last was said with a quick flicker of eye contact.

"And me?" Paul asked.

"Caroline was the first one missing that year. She was a couple years younger than you, and new to town," Cliff said. Paul remembered her as her name was spoken. New girl from out of town… wild red hair. "It was a cold March; snow still covered the ground. I thought it would be easy to track anyone, but the small prints I found in the field disappeared as they neared the forest. I spent days out there looking for sign of her. Like I said, it had been a few years, and I couldn't stand to think Red Creek was going to be that place where the sheriff's department let some pervert take the town's children. Not on my watch."

Paul saw Cliff's coffee was empty, and now he resorted to getting a hit directly from the flask. "She was gone. I was at the orchard too. I walked every inch of it, and that damned Conway Smith was so smug about everything. I could tell something was off. After a day out there, Sheriff

Oliver told me to back off. That I was making people anxious, and that the girl disappeared. We needed to spin it that her father from out of town must have taken her. That caused a real stir, with the guy getting arrested, but I knew better. By the time her father was released, everyone seemed to have forgotten the missing little girl. Everyone but her mother and me."

Paul felt horrible, knowing the man in front of him was right. He hadn't heard anything about Caroline after that first week. A new girl who vanished, to leave Red Creek as it had been. "You never found her, did you?"

Cliff shook his head and took a long breath. "Nope. When I was starting to get back to normal, you went missing."

The hair on Paul's arms stood up straight to hear his dreaded nightmares come to life. He had so many questions but held back, wanting to hear the events from Cliff's mouth. He had to force himself to breathe as his lungs seemed to forget how to work.

"It was early fall. School just back in session. I remember pulling over to the edge of the school yard that first day, watching all the kids running, playing, and screaming. Each yell had my eyes darting around, looking for an assailant. But it was only a school day. They were safe, or so I thought. I vowed to never let the Creek take another kid without someone paying for it, that morning." Cliff took another swig from his metal flask, passing it toward Paul, who shook his head. He didn't want a nip; he wanted to hear what had happened to him. "Suit yourself. I went back to the office after my shift and overheard old Oliver taking a call. I could tell it was serious, but when I stepped into his office, he stood and walked over to the door, shooing me out. The bastard wasn't even going to tell me about it."

"Tell you about what?" Paul asked, leaning forward

now, fingers intertwined on the wooden table.

"You. I followed him in my own car, down that gravel road leading to the orchard. I kept my distance, leaving my lights off. That was back when you could actually have your lights totally off in a vehicle. Oliver pulled up to that damned iron gate, Conway Smith standing there waiting for him like a ghost, wrapped in a white double-breasted suit. They chatted for a minute, me hidden down the next driveway, pine trees blocking me from view. I saw an envelope pass from Conway to Oliver, and my boss took off, back down the gravel road in the dim autumn evening light. He never saw me sitting there, and I don't know what came over me. I felt like I'd witnessed something unsettling, and my gut told me they were hiding a big secret.

"I drove off, knowing there was another road that stopped a quarter mile from their back fence. I was going to hop the son of a bitch and check things out. An hour later, I was climbing over the fence, almost ripping my pants off on the top of that barbed bastard. With a scratched leg, I hobbled through the orchard, smelling the sweet stench of unpicked apples randomly spotting the ground. The trees were picked clean, the Smiths already doing their job before the first frost came in and surprised everyone, like it tends to do out here.

"First, I came across the barn. At night, it set my nerves on fire. I felt like eyes were on me the whole time, but the Smiths didn't have surveillance then and still don't, as far as I'm aware. Too much ground to cover, I suppose." He stopped taking another swig, this time letting the last drop stall on the flask neck before he shook it, letting it fall into his open mouth. Paul hoped this wasn't normal morning behavior for the man he was going to confide in.

Paul stared silently, watching a man trying to rehash a day he'd probably worked hard at forgetting.

"Where was I?" Cliff asked.

"The barn," Paul prompted, thinking about the barn they had just broken into, and he understood the way Cliff felt that night.

"Right. The barn. Anyway, I felt like eyes were on me, and maybe it was an owl, or bats, but I could feel penetrating gazes on me as I crossed the tree lines and into the barn's vicinity. By now, the moon was getting high, on a near cloudless night. I don't remember where I put my car keys these days, but I remember that night, that moon, and the smell like it was yesterday. You ever have that?" Cliff asked.

Paul nodded, thinking about the night in college, down that alley, where the shadow followed him.

"Sure. I bet most people have. I pushed down the urge to leave and walked into the barn. But I found nothing. I half expected to see you tied to the wall, old Conway sitting on a stool watching you, but it was empty. Never found a thing. I kept moving. I knew there was an old house on the lot too, one a caretaker used to live in, but those were only rumors. I'd never seen anyone there, and it had probably been fifty years since anyone had been there. The place was run-down even back then, and I'm sure it's nothing but useless moss-covered wood now.

"It was a ten-minute walk from the barn, and I was panting by the time I got there, my initial adrenaline waning, and the fence scratches on my leg burning. I walked to the side window, and it was so grease-covered I had to wipe it with my sleeve to even see inside. Through the murky glass, I saw nothing moving, no light of any kind. But my gut was talking to me that night. I kicked the half-rotted door away, splinters flying inward with most of the door jamb. I cringed at the noise, but no alarms were raised, no sounds came from the direction of the Smith mansion.

"The inside was pitch black, and I was thankful for the small flashlight I kept on my belt. It was nothing fancy like the ones nowadays, but its small krypton bulb did the job. I searched it high and low, surprised to still find furniture there. Though it was mostly eaten away by moths and mice by that point, the roof had a large hole in it, enough so I could see that big moon hovering overhead when I looked that way." Cliff paused, stood up, and called to Gloria for a couple of waters.

Paul, while not quite ready to like the gruff older man, was starting to appreciate him, if only he would speed the story up. Paul's blood was coursing through his veins at the speed of light. He was on the verge of learning what happened, or at least getting a piece of the puzzle that would bring the whole picture to light.

Cliff got the bottled water and tossed one at Paul, who caught it deftly and spun the plastic top off with ease. "Did you see anything?"

"Nothing. The house was empty," Cliff said, and before Paul could tell him to get on with it, he raised a finger. "Or so I thought. I heard a noise. Softly at first, but as I stood there, forcing my ears to hear, to actually listen, I heard it a little clearer. It was coming from the basement. The grungy dirt-bottomed, moldy-smelling basement I'd already been through. I cautiously stepped down the rotten steps into that dirt room and listened again. The back of the room, there was a kind of whining noise and a light scratching maybe. I pulled my gun, ready to shoot a rabies-infested raccoon or protect myself from whatever might be holed up out there.

"The rest of the basement walls were concrete, but this one had wooden planks, telling me it might be a false wall. Seen them a couple times when someone's trying to keep an illegal hooch outfit under wraps or whatnot, only this was no hooch racket. It took some work, but I ripped that damned wall down where I saw a small seam, and I was right. Behind the hinged hidden opening in the wall was you. I guess you were about thirteen or so, but you looked like a little kid, dirty and crying.

"I came near you, telling you that everything was okay, but you started to freak out. You were looking behind me, and I turned so quickly, even shooting a round into the wall behind me. Goddamn it, that look on your face scared me. There was nothing back there but my own shadow." Cliff stopped, looking at Paul, as if trying to remember him as he'd found him that night.

Paul shivered when Cliff mentioned his shadow. That was probably what he'd been looking at. Maybe it wasn't Cliff's shadow he'd seen.

"Holy shit. Are you telling me you found me in a room in that old house at Granny Smith's Orchards? Buried behind a fake wall?" Paul felt light-headed, memories of trying to push out from behind a mental barrier. He'd heard of people repressing bad things that happened to them, but he couldn't remember anything like that; not a speck of it lingered in his mind.

"Yep."

"How did my parents not freak out? Why doesn't Beth know about it, or me, for that matter?"

Cliff shook his head slowly. "I don't know. Your parents were shocked to see you come home. I brought you there with Oliver, and he made me stay back at the car. Your mother shrouded you with a blanket and hugged you close, but when the sheriff came back, he told me that you were well enough to stay home. Didn't need a hospital. I argued with him about that, and he threatened to fire me if I talked back to him anymore. Also said they weren't pressing any charges."

"I can't believe this. Something's very wrong here in the Creek, Sheriff," Paul said, trying to imagine his hard-nosed mother consoling him.

"You were so scared. Shivering the whole way. Wouldn't even tell me your name. Didn't say a word. Conway knew you as the driver's kid. Only way we knew where to bring you. I've never seen anything like it."

"So how did they get away with it? You had me as proof!" Paul yelled, standing up and spilling his half-empty cup of murky coffee.

"They said you must have snuck into the orchard. They claimed teens did it all the time to drink beer or smoke weed. Said you were probably high and went into the old house to do some stupid stuff and got stuck in the basement. I know it's a load, but Oliver pressed me to shut my trap, and we never even filed a report. I was happy to have a missing child returned. A week went by, and I kept my eye on you. Your parents kept you from school; the rumor was you had a nasty flu bug. They drove you somewhere a few times, and eventually, you looked like a normal kid. I remember seeing you on a Thursday afternoon, face white, skittish, and the next time I drove to your street, you were riding your bike around with the Benning kid like nothing had happened. I began to think maybe everyone was right and you had gotten yourself into a mess, then were sick. The evidence proved me wrong, so I let it go but never forgot.

"It was a few years before we had another one disappear, and your face was the first thing I pictured. Only when I went against Oliver and got a warrant for the orchard, there was nothing to be seen at their mansion, the old house, or the barn. Clean as a whistle, so I digressed.

"Oliver had the big one about five years later, leaving me in charge. I poked and prodded around for details on the Smiths, but no one seemed to think anything odd of them. And they were the life-blood of the community, giving most of the Creek's tourism, tax money, and jobs. I let it be but never forgot, and here we are. I'm twenty years older, thirty pounds heavier, and much more cynical than that idealist ever could have thought." Cliff downed the last of his water, his voice growing scratchy. Paul guessed he wasn't one to give speeches very often.

"I owe you a huge thank you." Paul stuck out his hand. Cliff looked him in the eyes and clamped it in his own callused grip.

"Think nothing of it, son. You were probably the only reason I stuck with this job for so long. It was a shining moment for me, though no one ever knew about it. Sometimes those are the best ones. The glory of knowing you helped save a small life, when so many had been snuffed out over the history of Red Creek. Now if you know anything about this mess, tell me, because I've been thinking of retirement and I need to bust some heads before that happens."

Paul knew he couldn't just leave it behind. If he did, he would never have closure on his old home. He needed this just as much as the town did. Plus, that blonde temptress had drugged him, and that wasn't going to fly either.

"Something's bugging me, Sheriff," Paul said.

"Lots of things bugging me, son. What is it?"

"The cellar. What was their excuse for it?"

Cliff looked at him sidelong, thoughtful. "What cellar?"

"The one under the barn. We found my bike in there the other night."

"Son of a bitch, I knew it." Cliff slammed his palm against the oak table, making Paul jump slightly. "Tell me everything you can."

"You're never going to believe me when I tell you this stuff, and try to forget that I'm a horror author when you listen. Because Red Creek's been under a shadow for over a hundred years." Paul sat back down with a thud and started to talk.

Fifteen

"*I* want to see Dad," Taylor said in a tiny voice, almost a whisper. Her eyes were red and had dark bags under them.

"We're going now." Terri opened the door on Paul's old Land Rover, the one he'd bought with his first big advance and said he couldn't get rid of. The extra parking space alone was worth more than they made, the first few years together, but seeing it again still made her smile. Had they ever been that young and bright-eyed?

She slid the file folder off the luggage. She promised Don she'd bring a copy of the offer, since no one seemed to be able to track Paul down in Red Creek and the courier wouldn't drop it off without his signature.

"You ready? Do you have to pee one last time?" Terri asked, petting her daughter's freshly shampooed mop of hair. Taylor shook her head and got into the back seat.

Before Terri knew it, they were heading north on 9A, down the busy Manhattan street. It was an hour of construction and traffic jams before they emerged from what she called the city, and through Yonkers. Another bad night of sleep. Taylor had demanded all the lights be left on and had clutched her mom so hard Terri was sure bruises were beginning to form on her arms and back. Maybe Paul would have some insight. He'd always been a touchy sleeper; she didn't think it was a coincidence the man she'd married wrote a best-selling novel about shadow things and now their daughter was screaming she had been attacked by one.

She hoped it wasn't a hereditary brain disorder. Paul had said his mother was at Greenbriar, and that she wasn't herself any longer. Would that happen to Paul, then to her little girl? Was it already happening? Paul had often been aloof, head in the clouds, eyes glazed over like he couldn't hear a thing in the world. He always claimed it was his writer's brain churning, planning his book, but maybe there was more to it.

She peeked into the rear-view mirror and saw Taylor's eyes were closed, her head tilted back the way she did when she was out like a light. Finally.

Her dad's passing still only half registered with every-thing else going on. Taylor's fear; Paul's abrupt behavior and being in the hometown he'd vowed to her he'd never return to; the showings of the condo. The couple who'd made the offer seemed like assholes, the kind of rich trust-fund people that got married too young and resented each other but would lose the money if they ever separated. Terri snickered, thinking maybe she should write a book too.

Taylor still slept an hour later as Terri stopped and filled up with gas. The tank was running on empty, and who knew how old that gas had been? If she knew Paul, he'd added stabilizer to it, because that was the kind of man he was: thorough, almost to the point of annoyance at times. But still, as she leaned there pumping the fuel into the Rover, she thought about his brown hair, the little dim-ples he had when he shaved enough to see them, and the feel of his hands on her body.

Why had she ever left him? Because he couldn't write a book and he was going nuts? He had an angry streak but never hurt them, and she never felt threatened by him. He was so damned miserable all the time. Maybe she could have gotten a job and supported him for a while. She could have been at his side, making his life better, instead of pretending she deserved better and spending all her time at a yoga studio or a stupid spin class.

And taking his daughter across the country… it suddenly felt so foolish and horrible. Her reflection gazed back at her in the tinted windows, and she saw it was crying. The gas tank full, the pump snapped shut, and she hit the "no receipt" button when it buzzed at her.

The tears still fell silently as Terri pulled away: tears for her marriage and for her father. At least she'd said goodbye to him. He'd looked so frail there in a hospital gown, under a light blanket, machines softly beeping around the room.

Taylor still slept in the back as they drove, and the silent GPS said they were only thirty minutes from their destination. She could feel her nerves clench at being so close to seeing Paul again. Would he be angry? He'd sounded okay on the phone, like he missed her, and loved her, but would seeing her, the woman who left him and took his baby, set him off? He had every right to be mad.

Terri looked up from the GPS to see random two-by-fours on the highway. She slowed to avoid them, but something blew, and the car pulled to the side. She tried to breathe calmly as she depressed the brake and moved to the shoulder of the road.

"Mommy, what was that?" Taylor asked from the back seat.

"A flat tire, honey." Just what they needed. She looked at the clock; it was two in the afternoon.

***

*T*he pill bottle had still been in Paul's glove box, and he called the number printed on the small pharmacy tag. He was surprised to hear it ring on the other end, thinking it might have been disconnected after so many years. The kitchen at his mom's house was organized and cleaner than it had been in years, and he sipped a cup of coffee from the old brewer.

"Gilden General, Blaire speaking," a woman's voice answered.

"Do you know a Doctor Norman?" he asked, not knowing the man's first name, but wishing he did.

"Doctor Norman? No, I don't."

"Can you check your files? He was my doctor years ago, and I'm checking to see if he still practices." Paul wished his Google searches had come up with some re-sults. Apparently, the old-timer practiced pre-internet only.

"Hold please," she said, the line clicking, and tacky eighties pop songs took over. "Okay, Mr...."

What harm could it do? "Paul. Paul Alenn."

There was a pause on the phone. "Like the writer? Sorry, I'm sure you get that all the time. He's my favorite author. Even the newer ones."

Paul smiled. "Not as often as you'd think." Actually, he rarely got that, but here in Red Creek and Gilden, he might be somewhat of a hometown hero, one of the few people to leave and be interviewed by Regis Philbin. He laughed at how long ago that interview had been. "You like the newer ones, hey? Even *Locust?*"

"Oh, especially *Locust*. It was less about the plot than the main character's story and development. When she broke through the power of her awful past and killed those men... it was liberating."

He beamed as she spoke. This woman got him!

"Wait, are you really him?" she asked.

If it would get him personal information, he was happy to play along. "Yes, ma'am. In the flesh." The term crawled over his skin after he said it.

"Well, I'll be."

"About that address?" Paul asked, hoping this worked.

"I'm not really supposed to do this."

"Well, I could swing by tomorrow to sign a couple books if you like, Blaire." This seemed to get her excited, and he could hear her hemming and hawing, expressing her deep internal battle.

"You didn't hear it from me. And I'll see you tomorrow, right?" she asked.

"No one will know where I got it from. I have a question for him. Won't bug him for more than a couple minutes. And yes, I'll be there tomorrow." He hoped he could follow through with his promise. Very few people got excited about his books any longer.

He jotted down the address and the phone number she had listed for him, thanking Blaire one last time before ending the call.

Step one down. He Googled it, finding it in a rural area between Red Creek and Gilden. Bingo.

He stepped into the living room, where piles of boxes still overtook the space, brown carpet visible only if you looked hard for it. A stack of photo albums lay on one of the rows of boxes, the kind with ornate, gold-colored etched edging that you only saw at your grandparents'.

Paul didn't remember ever seeing them before, but he was learning there were a lot of things he didn't seem to remember about his childhood. He sat down on the one open chair left in the room and dialed Dr. Norman's home phone number. A voice recording blared back through his speakerphone, the voice that of an old man. He hung up before leaving a message. That conversation was going to be a strange one and would be better suited to a face-to-face anyway.

The picture album was full of old black and white photos, of people he'd never seen before. They were classic: families sitting on the front stoop of an old farmhouse, the old man in a rocking chair, wearing his finest wool suit. The kind of suit you knew would make a man sweat through his underwear in the heat of the summer, but they still wore them because their wives threatened to beat them with a broom if they didn't listen. He imagined the man in the picture to have a cup of whiskey under his seat and a mouth full of chewing tobacco. He had that look to him.

His wife stood with her thick-fingered hand on his shoulder. What was it about those old turn-of-the-century photos? All the adults had the weight of the world on their shoulders, miserable as all hell, and they all looked like they could play for the New York Jets – not just the men.

She scowled, dark hair tied in a severe ponytail, more layers than an onion covering her thick-boned body. Paul smiled as he looked at a moment of someone else's life. Terri had once complained that he couldn't take a good photo of her, and Taylor had spoken up, saying, "That's how you looked at that moment, Mom." It was pure gold, and they'd all had a good laugh at it.

Paul's smile quickly slipped from his face when he looked down to the endless row of rugrats sitting and standing before their parents. The girl second from the left looked so much like his mother, he almost dropped the book. It made sense that one of her ancestors would have looked like her, but it jarred him, since he'd never seen these photos before. He tried to think of who they could be and couldn't think of an answer.

The album had those plastic sheets that stuck to the

backdrop, so he peeled back an edge, the plastic making that noise it always did as he lifted it from the ancient book. It had probably sat in that spot for fifty years or so, and it cracked a little as he moved it.

The picture came free with ease off the yellowing page, and he flipped it around, heart pounding at what he might find. He was dreading it, but it also felt like something inevitable, like a plot in one of his books that he didn't see coming.

Written on the back in faded ink was: *The Smiths, 1906.*

He was related to the Smiths. And judging from the photo, it was on his mother's side, which made sense on the name. The cloudy picture of Red Creek and his shadow man was starting to come together: clues and parts falling into his lap, some upside down, and others missing corners.

His cell phone rang, and Terri's number appeared. She was probably quite stressed in the city, trying to work out the funeral details. He wished he could be with her to help, but he had to see Norman. He let it go to voicemail, grabbed Darrel's jacket and the good doctor's address, and left in a hurry. They had things to do that evening, and he didn't want to be late. He still had the photo in his hand, and he slid it into his back pocket. A stop at Greenbriar might be necessary too. Maybe his mom would be more lucid and could answer some questions – mainly, why she seemed to flip a switch from being mom of the year to a bitter hag so quickly. It was all tied to the orchard, he could sense it.

He wished that old bastard Sheriff Oliver was still around so he could go beat some answers out of him. Letting kids disappear and shoveling it under the dirt like a shallow grave digger. Paul hoped his heart attack had caused him immeasurable pain.

This time, as he drove by the path leading to the forest, he felt his heart pump faster: not in fear, but in anticipation of what was going to happen. He was going to face his fears, but he needed to know the details first. And Doctor Norman was the man to shed some light.

***

"You're going out again tonight? Tell me it's nothing dangerous," Beth said to her husband, who was calling from work. At least he'd finally gone in today. She was beginning to worry he'd lose his job.

"Paul called and said he needed us at seven o'clock. We're meeting at Chuck's," Darrel said from the other end of the phone.

She hoped Paul wasn't going to bring them into something that he couldn't get them out of. Red Creek didn't seem like the quiet, safe place it always had been. But when she thought about it, maybe it never was a quiet safe place. The whole town would go out searching for one of their own missing kids, and two days later, they would forget about it, like it never happened. At least it seemed like her brother was trying to figure it out. God knew the sheriff's department had never done anything to help it.

She thought about the time Paul had come back home in the back of the fat old cop's car, dirt covering his pale face, blood dried onto his ripped fingernails. Their parents told her Paul had gotten himself stuck in an old house in the forest, but when she grilled Paul about it a week later, he acted like she was crazy and shrugged it off.

Paul had acted so strange those few days, randomly screaming, and a minute later shuffling around like a zombie.

"Please be careful, okay? You coming home first?" she asked.

"Don't think so. I got a lot to do here, then I figured I'd grab a bite at Chuck's before we go. Or whatever we're doing."

"I love you, Dar," she said, trying to remember the last time she'd told him she loved him. It had been a few months.

"Love you too, Elizabeth," Darrel said, using her full name. He only did that when he was being thoughtful. She teared up a little as the call ended.

Beth looked at the clock. It was almost three in the afternoon, her shift at the bank over in ten minutes. Then it was off to the school to pick up Isabelle. Her phone buzzed again, on the counter, and she expected to see Darrel's image appear on the screen. Instead, it was an out-of-state number she didn't know. "Hello," she answered.

"Beth?" the voice asked.

"It's me."

"Oh, thank God. It's Terri. I can't get hold of Paul, and I'm just outside Red Creek with a flat tire. It looks like they can tow it, but they're a couple of hours away. I... didn't know who else to call," the voice said, sounding more frazzled than Beth had ever heard her sister-in-law.

"I'm about to leave work, and I have to grab Isabelle. Tell me where you are, and I'll be there in thirty minutes."

Terri gave her the approximate spot, and she knew the place. It was about a mile south of the truck stop that sat on the edge of the interstate and their side road. She was only a few miles from town, at most.

"I'll see you soon," Beth said, wondering when she'd last seen Terri and Taylor. It had to be at least four years. Taylor and Isabelle were only two little tykes, not in school yet.

A customer came in, and she put on a smile, and it was a dichotomy to the sinking feeling of dread growing in her belly.

Sixteen

*P*aul's car shot up a stream of dust as he raced down the gravel road leading to the doctor's house. At the sight of a driveway, he slowed, seeing a "The Normans" wooden sign swinging slowly in the increasing breeze. Black clouds were rolling in from the west, bringing what looked like a nasty autumn storm along with them.

The driveway was long but not gated like some of the others out in this area. Paul was thankful for the small things that went his way.

He approached the house, which was situated on a large plot of land, probably four or five acres if he was to guess. It was an old colonial and looked like it had been well taken care of. Paul appreciated the landscaping as he parked. This guy had probably done well for himself, though he was surprised a shrink in this area could even find clients. Money was hard to come by, and parting with it was harder.

His heart slammed against his ribcage as a large dog ran from behind the house, barking loudly, teeth flashing. It was a dark German shepherd, and Paul almost got back in his car when a sharp whistle raced through the air. The dog stopped on the spot, sitting down but still growling at him.

"Sorry about that. Thomas gets a little excited when we have visitors." The man was still in his doorway and had to be pushing eighty. What was left of his hair was pure white and sticking up in all directions.

"Good boy, Thomas," Paul said, stepping forward and sticking his hand out, which earned him a deep low growl. He quickly pulled it back and walked to the front porch, keeping an eye on Thomas the whole time. "Hello, are you Doctor Norman?"

The man raised a bushy eyebrow and nodded. "Henry. Henry Norman, yes. Though I haven't practiced in ten or so years, so Henry is fine with me these days. What can I do for you?"

It felt like there was some familiar aspect of the man, but Paul still couldn't recall having met him, though he must have if he'd prescribed those antipsychotics to a young Paul.

"My name's Paul Alenn. I think I was a patient of yours twenty-something years ago, though I honestly don't remember it."

The old man's lip twitched but snapped back into place a split second later. He was composed. "I don't think I ever treated you. I'm sorry."

"I think you did, Doctor Norman. I have a pill bottle here." He took out the bottle, turning the label to Henry. He was now at the bottom of the three steps leading to the porch, and Henry was only about five feet away.

"Oh, I'm sorry, my eyesight isn't what it used to be, but my partner used my labels a lot," the doctor said, shifting on his feet.

Paul wasn't buying it. "And where can I find your *partner?*"

"At the Red Creek Cemetery. Been dead fifteen years or so."

Great, the guy was playing hard ball. He'd assumed it was going to go something like this. He took a step up the stairs, and Henry stepped back at the same time, a look of fear crossing his wrinkled visage.

"I'm not here to hurt you. Far from it. I need to know what happened that autumn. The autumn of ninety-three. I know you treated me for something traumatic, and I have no memory of it. There's a bad thing happening in Red Creek, and you've got to tell me about it. You can help save lives." It sounded way too dramatic to Paul's ears, but he hoped the guy would bite. Hell, it was the truth.

A wave of resignation washed over the doctor's face, and he waved a thin arm, motioning Paul to come inside. "I've got a pot of coffee on. Doctor said I should cut back, but I'm eighty-two. If I can't enjoy a hot coffee during the day and a glass of scotch in the evening, then what was it all for?"

Paul was beginning to like the man. The house was well-kept. He probably had a maid service come through once a week, judging by the cleanliness. Pictures littered the walls, nice frames showing a happy-looking family through the ages. A picture of a young couple in black and white, holding hands, and the same couple every decade or so, posed much the same.

"She's beautiful," Paul said, smiling at the red-headed woman in the photos. He ached for Terri and wished he'd answered her calls. His family had never been close like the good doctor's here, but it hadn't always been so bad with his parents, and then with Terri. He was determined to salvage what he still could.

"She sure was. Met her at a fair. Can you believe it? Gilden used to have that summer fair every year. There would be a Ferris wheel, and they played movies on that big outdoor screen. We kissed for the first time on that wheel, yes we did," Doctor Norman said wistfully. "Sorry, I'm rambling, and you're here for another reason. We don't get much company anymore, I'm afraid." He petted

Thomas on the head, who was busy smelling Paul's feet.

"That's okay." Paul followed him past the living room and into an uncluttered kitchen – a large juxtaposition to his mother's house. A coffee pot was hissing out a little steam as the carafe filled up.

"Coffee?" the doctor asked.

Paul accepted, and they sat at the small eat-in wooden table.

"You do remember me, right?" Paul asked.

"I do. It was quite the case. Experimental stuff. You were the first and last person I ever tried that treatment with."

Paul felt scared and relieved to hear the man accept a part in his past. "What exactly was the treatment?"

The man waved a finger in the air and left the room, leaving Paul with a mouthful of coffee and questions. A few minutes later, he shuffled back in with one of those old beige file folders, Paul's name scrawled across the label tab in "doctor" handwriting.

"That's…?" Paul started to ask, but the doctor just nodded, cutting him off.

"This is it." Norman scanned the files, making "uh-huh" sounds and frowning a lot.

"What does it say?" Paul needed to know. Enough with the drama.

Doctor Norman set the file down and put his coffee cup on top of it. It was obvious the file was for his eyes only.

"It was a long time ago, but I'll never forget. I was younger, but still in the business for thirty-five years when your mom showed up at my door, begging for help. You were unlike anything I'd ever seen. At first, I thought sexual abuse–" He paused, as if trying to get a read on Paul, but got nothing but a poker face in return. "–but dismissed it eventually. You don't even want to know how often that came up over my career. Enough to make you question everything, that's for sure." He stopped, taking a drink of coffee, and Paul could feel the caffeine coursing through his veins. He wanted to prompt the old guy to keep going but didn't want to piss him off.

"At first, you wouldn't say anything, then you would start to scream about the shadows. I had to keep lights on all around the room, so they canceled out any chance of shadows on the floors. It was quite strange, but I'd seen a lot of mental illness, and the mind can do very tricky things when it wants to. You were here for a full day that first visit, your mother and father pacing around my living room or outside, worried like nothing I'd ever seen before. I sent you home that first day with some sedatives, and I worked that night on a plan. You had told me a crazy story, one about a man in black stealing you and locking you in a cellar, where you managed to escape and crawl through tunnels. I was told you'd snuck onto Granny Smith's, gotten lost and stuck in an old mine shaft."

Paul had never heard of a mine being in the area, but Norman didn't seem to be surprised by it. "Go on," he said.

"You were so scared. I'd never seen anything like it. You were also so confident that your story was true, but I bought in to the story your parents brought me. That you were apt to over-imagination, and this wasn't the first time something like this happened, though not quite to this extent.

"I mentioned an experimental theory I'd been working on. Hypnosis to forget something traumatic." Norman mopped his long face with a thin-fingered hand. "I only meant it to be a theory, and if ever used practically, it would be on an adult patient who mentally couldn't move on from a horrible traumatic event. I never meant to… you were just a child.

"They asked me to do it without hesitation. Right then, I should have rejected the idea. They were so adamant that I questioned what they were trying to cover up. I did turn them down that night, after an hour-long conversation that turned into more of a begging session from your mother."

Paul was leaning so far forward, he almost slipped from his seat. This was it. He'd been hypnotized. That would explain why he had no memory of that time of his life. The shadows of it had been following the rest of his life. Experimental, the doctor had said. What did that mean?

"They came back the next morning, with you a lighter shade of white, pupils dilated, and fear thick in your trembling voice. They handed me a check." Norman looked ashamed, posture not quite as straight as it had been. "If I said I didn't need the money, I'd be lying. I was a therapist outside a dying town, where people didn't talk about their feelings, and local insurance policies didn't allocate money to my type of doctor. But it wasn't the money that swayed me. It was your eyes." He turned and looked at Paul then, their faces two feet apart. "I see the same look in you now."

"How much was the check for? My parents had no money," Paul said, sure of that fact.

"Five thousand dollars. And it wasn't from your family. It was from Conway Smith." The doctor filled up his coffee cup again, offering more to Paul, who shook his head.

Conway had given Sheriff Oliver an envelope, and then paid for Paul's own hypnosis. And his parents were in on it. The family roots were deep on the orchard. He figured he'd been the first one to escape the orchard, thanks to Cliff, and they'd bought off whoever they needed to. Instead of killing Paul, they'd paid this old man to make him forget the whole thing.

"Are you close to the Smiths?" Norman asked, looking at Paul over his coffee cup as he sipped from it.

"No, but I think I'm beginning to understand a lot more. Tell me about that day," Paul said, legs fidgeting restlessly.

Doctor Norman cleared his throat. "I'd done hypnosis before, but nothing of this magnitude. The theory is, we can isolate a specific time period from someone's memory and add a block to it. It had been tested in the field many times; the most successful was having someone forget a whole day, but the block wore out after a week. I'd been reading about it a lot at that time, and thought I understood how to succeed where they failed. So you might say a selfish part of me wanted to test my theory out. I hadn't intended it to be for something of that importance, and definitely not for a paycheck for something I shouldn't be doing to a child.

"I believed a terrible event happened to you, but I didn't believe your story about a shadow creature dragging you there. More likely, it was a man. And the cover-up money by Conway led me to believe he was involved with it. I didn't have the facts, and the five grand sitting in my hand made my decision. I'm not proud of it, and I always wondered what happened to you."

Paul still sat silent, letting the man speak.

"Then I read your first book, *The Underneath*. It resonated so strongly with me, I feared my barrier broke, or leaked at the least. Shadow things dragging college kids to the Underneath, where they were tortured. It was so close to your story about being dragged into a cellar and tunnel, only your book was in a city. I almost phoned you a few times, but I let bygone be bygones. And here you are, so many years later, me an old man with an empty house and a mind full of regrets."

He sounded honest about everything to Paul.

"How did it work?" Paul asked.

"I convinced your parents to leave us alone. I hypnotized you, having you take me back to the moment you were thinking of leaving to ride your bicycle into the forest to meet your friend. I started from there. I tricked your mind into forgetting each event from then on; you described everything in detail. I couldn't believe how much your mind really believed what you were telling me. If I didn't know better, I would have actually thought you *were* taken by a shadow." Norman stopped, his voice getting raspy. "Paul, what do you think now?"

He wasn't one hundred percent sure. "I've seen it. Many times. Recently, too."

Doctor Norman looked shocked. "Can I give you my honest opinion?"

Paul nodded, wanting to hear what the man in front of him thought of the whole crazy scenario.

"Contrary to what your parents said, or what Conway Smith told the sheriff, I think someone did take you. This person has been taking children here for far too long for it to be one person, but I think it could be a copycat of some sort. I'm no police officer, but it's the only thing that makes sense. Most people around here get upset every time it happens, but they forget so quickly, and I don't understand that. I should have brought it to someone outside the town, but I didn't know who.

"At the end of the day, though, I think your mind was confused by the trauma, and you were lucky that Cliff found you when he did. I suspect you would have died down there, at the hands of a monster. A human, but a monster nonetheless. You created this shadow man as an explanation, because you didn't understand how a person could do that to a little boy. Maybe you even knew your captor. When I made you forget, you rememebered the shadow aspect of the trauma, and since you say you've seen it over the years, that's just part of the hypnosis leaking out." Doctor Norman drank the last of his cup of coffee, setting it down and pushing it across the table. "That's my theory, at least."

It made sense to Paul. It really would explain a lot. It seemed like one of his ancestors must have been a serial killer. The family kept it secret, and the killer passed his ideologies on to another, who followed after him. Children were still being killed, and they would have to be on the fourth generation at least. But Terri said Taylor had seen a shadow monster, and Darrel had seen one too. Paul had never told them about it. Darrel would know what his book was about, and he was sure Taylor had seen the movie based on his novel by now. He could see her watching it in a friend's room, streaming on a tablet under a blanket. It would explain a lot, but Paul wasn't buying it.

"There's only one way to find out. Doctor, I want you to remove the block." Doctor Norman paled when Paul said it. "Give me my memories back."

Seventeen

Cliff ate his hamburger as he always did, in his sheriff's car, watching Main Street. He pictured his wife driving by, admonishing him for eating the heart-clogging burger. Truth was, she was probably right about it. He did need to straighten up and start taking better care of himself. He used to run a few times a week and play on the town softball team, but he'd given all of that up a long time ago. Red Creek had a way of killing ambition; he knew this now.

It was his life, though, and it was time to stop sitting on the sidelines. "Put me in, coach. I'm tired of riding the pines," he said to himself.

He looked down at the foil-wrapped food in his hand, and decided he was done with that crap. He wrapped it up and tossed it back in the bag with Chuck's restaurant logo on the front. When this was all over, he'd go home and shave, shower, and give his wife the attention she deserved.

The clock shone 4:06 PM, and it was getting closer to the time. Paul Alenn had surprised him. It was hard to believe this guy was the same person as the dirty little scared boy he'd pulled from the basement of that house so long ago. He hated leaving the rest of his tiny department out of the loop on his plans, but he honestly wasn't sure if he would trust them to back him against the Smiths. The whole town was under Conway's thumb.

Paul's theories were sound. They would find evidence

tonight of the missing kids, and it would all end. The old man would go to prison, if he didn't die of his cancer first, and the town could start fresh, with a massive black cloud lifted from overhead.

He also hated needing to rely on Jason Benning and Darrel, but his plan was to deputize them to keep things on the up and up. Paul too, for that matter. Hell, he'd deputize the whole lot of them if they woke up tomorrow with the orchard under wraps.

Cliff had a lot to do still before meeting the guys at Chuck's at seven. A car drove by as he turned the ignition. Beth from the bank was at the stop sign, driving a woman he didn't recognize; two little girls were in the back seat. He locked eyes with the one that didn't belong to Beth. They were sad eyes, and they stayed on him as the car pulled away.

***

*B*eth took a frozen pizza out of the oven and slid it onto a pizza tray. "Sorry, this is all I have."

Their reunion had been a tear-filled one, with Terri so relieved to see someone she knew. Taylor was still upset over whatever she'd seen the other night, and Terri had hardly slept a wink herself since then. Add in the planning of her father's funeral and being the executor of his will, and she was ready to drop from exhaustion and heartbreak.

"That's totally fine with us. Right, Taylor?" she called to the other room, where she could see the top of her daughter's head. The girls were watching some cartoon. Isabelle was singing along to the songs, while Taylor sat quiet and subdued. They needed to see Paul. She needed her husband's warm embrace, and their girl needed her father.

"I'm sorry we haven't been a part of your lives. I was selfish for leaving Paul like that." She kept her voice low so Taylor couldn't hear.

"It goes both ways. I could have picked up a phone too," Beth said. Terri had always liked her sister-in-law and could see the resemblance between her and Paul.

"So tell me what's been going on here. Paul hasn't been very clear, but I'm worried. He hasn't seemed himself."

Beth turned the timer on for the oven and sat down heavily. She looked as tired as Terri felt. "You know about the history of Red Creek?"

Terri shook her head. "Paul never really talked about it."

"Well, children have been disappearing here as far back as the county has been here. Some adults too, but those are easier to explain. Paul, Jason, and Darrel went to the records office and made a list of everyone missing over the years." Beth's eyes were wide. Terri's heart was speeding up. She couldn't believe she didn't know any of this about Paul's hometown.

"Before you go on, how about that glass of wine?" Terri felt her nerves begging for something to calm them down. Truth be told, she wanted something a little stronger than a merlot after this week, but she happily accepted the three-quarters-full glass of cheap wine. Beth poured herself a slightly less-full one.

"According to Darrel, Paul thinks it all relates to Granny Smith's Orchard. He was over there the other night..." Beth paused, as if realizing she shouldn't have said something.

"What is it?" Terri asked, the wine already hitting her and her empty stomach.

"Oh, he went over there to take Katherine Smith on a date." Beth blushed but quickly came back. "It wasn't anything like that, don't worry. Paul isn't interested in her, though Darrel couldn't stop mentioning how attractive she is. But that's my oaf of a husband, not yours. I don't know what happened, but Darrel talked to him today."

A date. She couldn't really blame Paul. She'd been on a few dates in California, but never anything serious. Terri wasn't ready to hear her husband was moving on. Especially since he'd told her he loved her the other day. And he probably did love her, just as she still loved him even when she moved away, but often love morphed from the passionate to the comfortable and caring.

"It's fine. It sounds like he was doing it for a reason," Terri said, only half believing herself.

"The guys broke into the orchard and my stupid husband ended up shooting Jason in the arm."

"What?" Terri exclaimed, loudly enough to make both girls look back.

"It's okay, honey. Watch your movie," Beth said with an admonishing look at Terri. "They went looking for Tommy O'Brian. He went missing the day after Paul arrived."

So much had happened, and Terri was only hearing about it now. Why hadn't Paul been more forthright with her? "Did they find him?" she asked.

Beth slowly shook her head before taking a small sip of wine. "No. But they found something in an underground room under the barn."

Terri almost slid off her chair, she was leaning forward so far. "What was it?"

Beth leaned closer to her, and Terri could smell the cheap wine on her breath. "Paul's bicycle from when he was a kid."

Terri's mind reeled with the news. It didn't make any sense to her, and she knew she was only seeing a few random snippets of the full picture. "How did Jason get shot, then?" she asked, her hands trembling.

Beth rolled her eyes. "Darrel got spooked by a shadow."

Terri's heart pounded, and she looked to make sure Taylor hadn't heard that. It didn't look like she had. "What do you mean, a shadow?" Her voice was quivering.

"He told me he didn't care what Jason thought. He saw a shadow figure down there with them, and it was coming for his friend, so he shot at it but hit Jason instead, and it was gone, just like that. Paul came down as it happened, and I'm sure he caused the shadow somehow, even though Darrel claims he couldn't have, since there was no light behind him. Anyway, my husband shot his buddy. But why Paul's bike was there is beyond me."

Beth was telling the story like it was no big deal, but Terri could hear the fear behind her voice.

"Where's Paul now? Darrel must know." Terri was getting too anxious to be sitting around a kitchen table while her husband was running around chasing his shadow.

"I have no idea. Darrel doesn't either. He told them to meet at Chuck's at seven. That's their other friend. He owns the only decent restaurant in town. If I heard correctly, old Sheriff Cliff is finally on board, and he's going with them tonight." Beth got up and spun the pizza tray inside the oven.

At least now Terri knew where they were going to be. She picked up her phone and dialed Paul's number again, with Beth watching her silently. Damn. Voicemail. "You said the sheriff was going with them. Going with them where?"

"To the orchard."

The buzzer on the timer went off, startling Terri. Isabelle ran into the room.

"Pizza!" she called. Taylor trailed after her, eyes puffy. She came and stood nestled up to Terri, and she wrapped her arms around the girl's small body.

"Let's eat, then go find Daddy," she said to her daughter, and for the first time in days, she got a smile in return.

***

Paul woke again, still in the musty dirt-walled room. His head throbbed, and he wondered if he had a concussion. Billy at school had one last spring, and he said he wasn't supposed to sleep. Paul worried he'd made himself worse off by passing out.

The lantern was still on, a tiny glow coming from the oil-deprived wick. He needed to find a way out. For the first time in his young life, he feared he might die. Kids worried about things like that when they learned about death, but most didn't come face to face with the distinct possibility of it. Paul faced it now as he stood, dizzy-headed, and felt along the hard-packed wall. Everything was stiff on him. Sleeping on the floor in the fetal position hadn't been great for his back or legs. Trying to remember what his phys-ed teacher said, he stretched his back and legs in opposite movements to their resting position, countering the strain.

His stomach growled, but he put that to the back of his mind. He could eat later; right now, he just needed to survive. To escape.

He felt around the door, looking for a release somewhere, but couldn't find anything but splinters. He ran his hands on the bottom of the wooden slab, not even enough room to slide a pinky underneath. Paul focused his efforts on the walls. He closed his eyes and pictured the room as it had been when he first woke up there. The lantern had been bright. The far wall was a different color than the other three. He moved to that side of the small room, and it smelled musty as he approached. It wasn't the same. The dirt was wet when he touched it, not rock hard like the others. It was newer. Maybe freshly dug! He went to it, digging his hands and fingers into it. He was able to make a small hole, and he kept clawing away.

It was at least a half hour later when he heard something from outside the room. He stopped moving, trying to keep his frantic breath under control. He willed himself to let the thing think he was still sleeping. The lantern was dark now, and he could only see the barest hint of an outline under the door.

Paul pressed his back against the wall, facing the doorway, seriously wondering if his heart would explode before the shadow man killed him. Whatever he'd heard was gone. He stayed still for another five minutes, tears pouring down his dirty face the whole time.

When he thought the coast was clear, he turned back and kept digging, sharp pain shooting from his exhausted fingers. When he was about to give up, his brain telling him he was wasting his energy on a hole to nowhere, he felt his arm push through into air. He'd made an opening!

Hope coursed through him, and two minutes later, he had a space large enough to crawl through. But to where? The tunnel was pitch black too, and he had no idea what was in there. It was either that or staying a sitting duck in a small room. He wasn't going to play dead; he was going to escape.

Paul wiggled through the dirt opening and into the tunnel. He wished he could cover his hole up, but there would be no wondering where he'd gone if someone went into the room. He felt the walls and found he could stand, the dirt ceiling two feet above his head. He ran a hand along it and beside him. Looking back, he thought he heard something. He had to be quick.

The memories flooded back into his mind like a torrential downpour of emotion. He could almost taste the dirt-caked salty tears from that day now, sitting on the chair in Doctor Norman's kitchen. He was shaking so badly he knocked his cup off the table, glass shattering, a jarring noise in the otherwise silent room.

"What was that?" he said, his own voice surprising

himself.

The doctor looked worried, and he passed Paul a napkin. At first, Paul didn't know why, but then saw the blood on the table before him, his nose leaking in a steady drip. He got up, brain still reeling from the dump of information. He had to get to the orchard and stop this. Using the kitchen sink, he washed his face, the bleeding seemingly stopped.

"Paul, I'm guessing it worked?" the doctor asked, smiling in spite of himself.

"Damn right it worked. How…never mind. I don't hold it against you, Doc. Thanks for helping me when I was a kid. I don't think I could have survived if you hadn't suppressed this from me." Paul meant it. The feelings he got twenty-something years later from the memory were enough to make him want to stick his head in the sand. That, or get a big bottle of whiskey and drown himself in it. Yes, he was thankful for what the man had done.

"You don't know how much that means to me, son. I've regretted not giving you real help, and the guilt of doing it for a check from someone responsible…" Norman stopped, looking at Paul with a serious pensive stare. "Was it Conway?"

Paul thought about it. In the memory, he did see a shadow man, but maybe it was his way of dealing with it. It very likely had been Conway the whole time. It was the only thing that made any sense. His memory of the traumatic event could have been altered in his own mind.

"I think so. Could my brain remember something that wasn't really there? Could I have substituted a monster in place of a bad man?" he asked.

Doctor Norman nodded slowly, as if calculating the odds of that being possible. "Definitely. I always thought that was exactly what you'd done. I should have gone to the police back then."

"I'm not sure it would have done any good. Thank you for your help."

"Don't thank me. Do stop by another time, when you figure it all out. It was nice to have company," the man said, and Paul's heart went out to the lonely guy.

"I will. And I'll bring a bottle of scotch with me." This got a smile, and Paul almost ran out the door. He checked his watch; it was six o'clock and the clouds had thickened, starting to spurt rain down over the county.

He had to get to Chuck's, but first, he needed to make a stop. The rain came down harder as he entered the Red Creek limits. The memory of that day ran through his mind over and over. He'd thought once he had that time back, he'd understand the full picture, but he found he had more questions than ever.

The roads were quiet, most people done with work for the day and at home making dinner or watching the evening news. He pulled into the parking lot at Greenbriar and found it to be mostly empty. He took a spot close to the door and ran from the car into the entrance, still getting soaked in the small amount of time.

Soft elevator music played through their speakers, and the front desk was vacant. Judging by the place, not many visitors came at dinner time. But Paul remembered where his mother's room was, so he strode down the hall, trying to not look out of place, and dreading the conversation. He needed answers and was sure she knew. Somewhere deep in her mind, she knew what was going on; he needed her to be there for him today.

Her door was ajar. Sounds from the small television in her room echoed through the doorway as he slowly pushed it open. Helen sat on her chair, looking even skinnier than she had the other day, if that was possible. Her gray bathrobe was cinched up tight, and it appeared to be two sizes too large for her tiny frame.

His memory of being trapped in the cellar room flooded back, and the feeling of wanting his mother came with it. What had happened to the two of them?

She looked from the TV to him, her eyes flashing a spark of recognition. He quickly crossed the room, enveloping the near stranger in his trembling arms. The boy inside him held her tight, tears falling freely for her... for their broken relationship.

"Paul," she whispered. Her thin fingers ran over his head in a gesture he remembered from his childhood. That only brought the tears out more, and his heart ached at the missing twenty years with his family.

"Why? Why did this happen to us?" he asked once his voice was almost under control. Paul wasn't sure how lucid she would be, but at the least he had a moment, a tender hug with his estranged mother, and he hoped it was as valuable to her as it was to him.

"How much do you know?" The question came out so smoothly that Paul blinked and held her at arm's length. She stared hard into his eyes, tears filling her own.

"I saw Doctor Norman. That much I know."

Her eyes widened, but she nodded. "It's probably time you know. I've fought myself for years, wanting to talk to you about it, but also wanting to leave it buried. But as the years went on, I missed you more and more, and the children kept disappearing. I had protection for Beth and Isabelle, but not Taylor, so you could never come to Red Creek."

At the mention of his daughter, Paul wanted to shake her to get answers out, but he held back, heart pounding as he waited for her to continue.

"What do you mean, protection? Against who?" he

asked, trying to keep his voice low.

His mom looked at him with clear eyes. "Our family's bane."

"Who's Timothy?" he asked, thinking back to the name of missing children on his list. Timothy Caldwell had gone missing in 1957.

Her voice caught in her throat, and for a second, he thought she was choking. "How do you know that name?"

"I made a list of all the missing people over the years. It was on there. Was he your brother?"

She nodded. "We were supposed to be protected, but one of us had to be strong enough to contain it. Conway's father had a heart attack, and it went for one of our own. The sacrifice was supposed to be enough for a hundred years. Or at least that's what we thought... until it took you."

He could hardly hear; his heart beat thick in his ears. "What is it?"

She touched his face, her hand soft and chilled. "A nightmare. One that won't go away. I had to keep you away, Paul. Don't you see now? I loved you more than anything, so I had to keep you away from it."

The fights she'd had with him, almost kicking him out of the house even before he graduated; it had all been to save him. But save him from what? The Smiths? Conway? Or was his memory of the smoking shadow a real representation of the evil over Red Creek?

"I'm sorry too, Mom." He leaned in, kissing her on the forehead, holding her face in his hands. "I missed you. So there's something living at the orchard, and your family is bound to it? How do we stop it?"

She looked about to reply when she turned and looked out the window. "Ben, is it time for dinner?" she asked, her voice lighter than it had been.

Ben? Wasn't he the orderly from Greenbriar? Paul looked to the door, but it was still closed. "Damn it," he whispered under his breath. "Mom, stay with me."

"Gerry, take the lasagna out of the freezer," she said, calling Paul by his father's name.

"No, Mom. Talk to me. Stay here, please," he begged, feeling the overwhelming emotion of her mind slipping away. Maybe she would come back. She could still help him figure this out.

He stayed for another ten minutes, holding her hand, but when his phone vibrated, he checked it, seeing it was ten to seven. They would be waiting for him soon. He opened the door, the smell of cafeteria food wafting down the halls. He escorted her into the dining room; a man in a white jacket came over and took her off Paul's arm with a smile.

"Goodbye, Mom," he said, but she was lost in herself.

Whatever he found under the orchards, would be taken down tonight.

Eighteen

"*A*nd that's it. You guys are now officially Red Creek deputies." Cliff passed them old badges he'd found at the station. They were probably from the sixties, but it didn't matter. It was more for show than anything.

The diner was closed for a special event, according to the sign Chuck set in the window, and Cliff was surrounded by Darrel, Jason, Chuck, Nick, and Tyler. A special event, all right. He hesitated as he saw the last two holding rifles. They didn't seem particularly bright, especially Nick, but desperate times, and all of that.

"Where the hell is Paul?" he asked, not expecting an answer.

"He's on the way. He just texted me." This from Alenn's brother-in-law, Darrel.

Relief flooded Cliff. He didn't know why, but something about Paul being there was needed. He could feel it, like a gut instinct he rarely had as a cop, but it was the same feeling from the day he found Paul in that basement, crawling out of the hidden room, face covered in dirt.

"How are we going in? Storming the front gate?" Jason asked, his face as grim as it had been the week after his son had gone missing.

"You and Darrel are going back to the hole you fools cut in the fence. I'll bring Chuck to the gate and keep these two—" Cliff waved his thumb at Tyler and Nick. "– as our personal bodyguards. I'll get them to let me in and wave this warrant at the sick old man." He really didn't want those two guys running around by themselves with guns.

"Is that thing legit?" Jason asked, his chin lifting toward the piece of paper.

"Hell, no. I found one online and doctored it a bit." They looked at him with surprise. "What? I ain't just another pretty face, gents. I think Conway and that blonde might be smart enough to call a lawyer, but I hope we can get to the bottom of it before then. We only need proof. Proof there are bodies under the floor of that house, or that barn. You two are going to find it, with Paul alongside you. He has to be there." The last was said quietly, through a clenched jaw.

Darrel set a knapsack on a table beside them. He pulled a headlamp out, and Cliff saw it had one of those little cameras the surfers and rock climbers used. These guys were on the ball. He hadn't even thought of that.

"Good work. Now remember, if you stumble on a grave down there, don't touch it. Take your video, and we'll have the proof. I don't want anything messing up the impending investigation more than my phony search warrant."

Chuck brought out some food for them all. He noticed Nick and Tyler digging right in, like their small brains couldn't comprehend they were going into some potentially dangerous shit in half an hour, but he let them eat. Cliff even picked at a few fries, knowing he was going to change his diet and life after tonight. Whatever happened, a new sheriff was going to be born in Red Creek.

"You think Conway did it?" Jason asked, eyes as intense as a bull's.

Cliff watched how he answered the question. Paul had spilled quite the tale out about his abduction coming back to him, and his missing memories of it all. He didn't want to believe the man, but his look as he told the story convinced Cliff of one thing. Paul had obviously believed what he said, and that was enough for Cliff. There very well could be some demon living there. Conway was only a man, made of blood and guts. The world was a messed-up place, and Red Creek fit the mold to a T.

There was a knock on the door, and Cliff saw Paul hopping from foot to foot as he waited out in the rain. Nick ran to unlock the entrance, and Paul clambered in, shaking his head like a wet dog. He didn't say anything; instead, he walked to the counter and grabbed a hamburger, taking a big bite. They all stood there, watching him devour the food: a man who apparently hadn't eaten in a month, judging by the way the ketchup dripped down his chin.

"You look like a man eating his last meal," Tyler said, turning beet red after he must have realized what implications that held.

Paul shrugged it off, and Cliff liked him more for it. "It's been a taxing day, and the last thing I want is to make poor decisions because I have low blood sugar. Toss me a beer, Chuck," Paul said.

"Are you sure that's a good idea?" Cliff asked him as another pair of headlights shone through the front windows.

"If you had the afternoon I did, then you'd agree. It's the best idea I've ever had," came the reply.

The door chime rang, and Cliff was about to curse Nick for not locking it behind them. The last thing anyone needed to see was the town sheriff standing around with this group, guns lining the diner countertop.

A woman ran through. "Paul!" she called, rushing at the group. "Taylor's gone! Someone took our baby!"

Red Creek

***

*P*aul dropped the last remaining bite of his hamburger and ran toward his wife. She was drenched, and he embraced her as she sobbed in his neck, rain and tears intermingling on his skin. "What do you mean?" he asked, blood rushing through his body at insane speeds.

"We left Beth's to come here. Darrel said he was meeting you here, so I had to see you. As soon as we got here, she got out of the back seat." Terri was yelling as she spoke, her voice a higher octave than Paul had ever heard from her. He noticed Beth and Isabelle outside, looking around, searching in the rain for Taylor.

"I got out of the vehicle no more than five seconds after her, I swear! And she was gone. We looked everywhere!"

Paul thought to his mother's words. *I had protection against Beth and Isabelle, but not Taylor…*

The old Paul would have felt panic at this, but the new one, with Red Creek back in his life alongside his memories from that autumn when he was thirteen, felt rage. It coursed through him, threatening to burst out like a bomb.

For the first time, he really looked at his wife since she'd arrived. Her hair was shorter than it used to be, and her face was wet with tears and rain; mascara ran down her pink cheeks. His hand slid behind her head, pulling her into his protection from the world.

"I know where she is, and I'm going to bring her back," Paul said, the other men puffing up at his words. It felt good to have friends in this situation. Last time, he'd been there alone.

"I'm coming with you," Terri said.

191

"You can't. It's too dangerous. Stay here at Chuck's. Keep the doors locked." He then whispered something into her ear. "Protect Beth and Isabelle. They're family."

She looked up at him, her eyes wide, but her jaw was set in grim determination. She nodded. The other guys were already heading for the door, taking two vehicles.

"I love you, baby," Paul said at last and gave her a quick but passionate kiss – not forgetting that Taylor was gone, but letting it fuel his emotions. "She'll be coming home to you tonight. I promise you that."

Terri kept holding his hand as he grabbed a shotgun, not knowing what good it would do if he really was up against a shadow. He'd done days of researching shadow mythology as he wrote *The Underneath,* and one thing remained constant: he had no idea how to kill them. He penned them in as evil spirits who dissipated when their original bones were burned to ashes. With a shrug, he grabbed a box of matches from the countertop and shoved them into his pocket.

Paul looked back as he stepped through the door, and Beth said something to him he couldn't hear because of the pouring rain and the blood thrumming in his brain. She locked the door, and Paul hopped into the passenger seat of Jason's truck. Darrel was in the back seat, looking nervously at him.

"What do you think we'll find tonight?" he asked.

Paul thought about his answer first. "The shadow that hangs over your home. That's what we're going to find." The answer hung there, no one speaking as Jason drove down Main Street before cutting off to the side roads that would lead north, out of Red Creek proper. The wipers were on their fullest setting, splashing rainwater to the sides, the rain never slowing as they approached the orchards. He thought he saw lights in the mirror a half mile back, but they were gone now. Probably a farmer heading back from out of town.

Jason threw the truck in park, taking his seat belt off. "We make for the barn. We go down the stairs and find evidence that children have been abducted here. That's all, according to Cliff."

Paul laughed, a hysterical cry that threatened to push out after this week in Red Creek. Was he going crazy? Did the floodgates of his memory block being opened only add to it? He closed his eyes, taking a breath, and saw himself sitting in place of his mother at Greenbriar, his eyes hazy and distant as he stared out the window. Beside him, a picture of Taylor sat... not a grown-up version like she would be, but seven-year-old Taylor, cute as a button, smiling wide for the camera.

"Paul, did you hear me?" his old friend said, shaking him from his reverie.

"I'm going to the little house first. You guys go to the barn. If you see Taylor..." Paul paused, taking a deep swallow. "Protect her with your life. Please."

They nodded, and Darrel clapped him on the shoulder. "Paul, I think we should stick together."

"There's a tunnel under the orchard, or there used to be. An intricate maze no one knows about. That room we were in the other night had a tunnel from it that leads through. There are a lot of *rooms* down there, and you'll find what you need in some of them. I can only imagine what they look like now." Paul opened the door, letting rainwater splash on his pants.

"How do you know this?" Jason asked, his skin pale.

"I was there. I was under the orchards when I was thirteen. *It* took me." He got out, running for the fence, leaving behind questions being shouted at him from the two men still in the truck. He didn't have time for answers now.

He had to find his daughter.

The fence they'd cut open wasn't quite mended, but they had tied it closed with a thin yellow twine, which he cut through easily with a box cutter he had stored in his back pocket. The other guys were catching up to him as he climbed through the opening and set his foot on the orchard grounds. Paul pointed them in the barn's direction and beelined toward the house, hoping his gut feeling was right. That was where he would find Taylor: in the large underground room, steps from the basement of that shithole.

Looking back, he saw the bouncing of a flashlight as his friends ran to the barn, headlamps jostling with the movement. He felt his forehead and realized he'd forgotten to grab one of the headlamps. He had a small LED keychain light in his jeans and he hated to think that was going to be his only light.

The sky would normally have given some illumination at seven thirty, but the heavy black clouds absorbed any light approaching from above, making the field of leafless trees feel like it was a graveyard at midnight, each bare tree a gravestone for a missing child. He had to make sure his baby girl didn't end up under one of them.

Paul's left foot caught an exposed root, and he tumbled to the ground. With a thud, he slammed into the grass, sharp pain shooting into his left side at the fall.

Cursing under his breath, he forced himself to get up. Leaves stuck to his jacket and he brushed them off with his right arm, which was no worse for the wear. Standing up straight, his back cracked, and his shoulder protested as he tested it out with a rotation of his arm, like a slow windmill.

His thoughts drifted to the new self he'd been about to embark on less than a week ago. He'd started a new book, was going to sell his place to make a new life, and was working on getting back into a jogging routine again. A few days later, all of that had fallen apart, but thinking about his lips touching Terri's made it all okay. It gave him the resolve he needed to keep moving, to finally face the demons he needed to.

Taylor was here, at the orchard, somewhere. The sense that she was being used to lure Paul back wouldn't shake from the front of his brain. He was the one that got away, and they'd done their best to bury it, to bury his memory of it, but he was back, and he remembered it all.

The house came into view. It wasn't much more than a shell of a home now; its frame standing, walls partially erect, the roof almost entirely weathered away. His new memory of that day had him comparing his thirteen-year-old self's recollection of it, safe in then Deputy Cliff's arms, being carried away from a nightmare by a man who didn't understand the half of what was going on underneath the ground.

Paul's moans and cries from that day felt like they lingered in the thin air as he approached the structure. No longer would his mind think of it as a house. It didn't deserve the connection to a home. It was a portal, a gateway to a horrible place. He unslung the shotgun from his back and held it in two hands, ready for whatever he found, but he still didn't know for sure if it was a monster of flesh and blood, or just a monster.

The door was ajar, and as he walked inside, rain still splattered against his head where the roof was missing, rotted out and lying on the floor he was stepping on. The smell was awful, moldy, and he resisted the urge to gag as he made his way across the rubble-strewn living room, and to the back set of stairs.

They'd seen better days. Even back then, the place had been in shambles. Now he was worried he'd have no way to safely get to the basement. But he found the stair edge was still there, mounted to the sturdy wall.

"They don't build 'em like this anymore," he muttered under his breath as he balanced his feet on the edge, holding his gun with his sore left arm, and pushing against the far wall with his right.

"Looky what we have here," a voice called from the entrance of the place.

Paul's heart jumped into his throat and he almost biffed it, his right foot losing grip. He managed to keep on his knees, instead of slamming his face onto the top stair and falling the fifteen feet below.

"Told ya we was gonna find Mr. Fancy Pants with his hand in the honey jar, Buck." Two men sauntered in; rain soaked them, a heap of damp plaid and denim vests. He knew the clowns from the liquor store the moment he saw them.

The short one, with the same trucker hat on, wielded a baseball bat in his hands, slapping the meat of it against his palm, trying to look intimidating. The lanky one smiled, gap-toothed, and the smell of stale whiskey mixed with the rotted wood, leaving Paul to grimace as he got to his feet.

"What in the hell do you two want?" he asked, annoyed at the inconvenience. Normally, he would be scared by two hillbillies intent on kicking his ass, but at that moment, knowing they were delaying him from finding Taylor, he was quickly sliding into a white-hot rage.

Fingers tingling, he lowered the shotgun, and that was when he saw the tall one pull out a handgun of his own.

"What do we want? We want to take down the Red Creek killer, that's what we want," Lanky said.

"Then what are you doing pointing a gun at me?" Paul asked, knowing their answer.

Shorty spat a load of chewing tobacco gunk out the

side of his mouth, brown liquid dripping down his chin. "The way we see it, you show up, and the O'Brian kid goes missing. You find the shoe with blood, trying to be some hero, but the way I see it, you missed it draggin' his little corpse over here, so you went to make sure you were the one to grab it. Where you keep the bodies? Down there?" He motioned for the basement, eyes wide and alert. If Paul was going to guess, these guys were hopped up on more than whiskey and chewing tobacco. "You some sort of perv, Mr. Fancy Pants? Move out the way, drop the gun, and we'll take care of the rest."

"I don't have time for this shit," Paul muttered, his gut willing him to fire on them, his brain the only thing holding him back.

Before he could register it, the lanky one was coming for him, while the short one was trying to move in from the other side. He could only shoot one of them, they probably thought. Not best logic for any sane person.

Instead, Paul swung the shotgun, the butt end clubbing Lanky in the throat. He went down, clutching his neck as the bat arced down toward Paul from Shorty's meaty grip. He ducked and tried to roll, but slipped, and he was soon sliding backwards and down the stairs that weren't really stairs any longer. His arms reached for anything to grab, but he fell. For a split second, he felt nothing but air against his back; then solid ground rushed at him, knocking the wind from his lungs.

His head swam as he looked up, Shorty smirking to himself like a fool. Paul stayed still, trying to assess the damage done to him, but didn't think it was anything too serious. The guy spat again, this time directed at Paul. Good thing his aim was as bad as his baseball skills.

"Stay there. Buck, get the cuffs. We're gonna be town heroes."

Lanky was getting to his feet, still coughing in pain.

Paul closed his eyes for a second, the room so dark he could hardly make out their forms any longer. Something shuffled beside him, and he knew it was time to get active. With a push from his sore legs, he sat up against the wall at the bottom of the stairwell.

For a moment, everything in front of him was black, and the next he could see Shorty, pulled to the side and out of sight. A sharp blood-curdling scream filled the room, and Lanky started to fire his gun, sparks glowing in the dark space with each round.

Not wanting to see what they were up against, Paul ran for the edge of the basement, climbing over wood and rotten furniture. The smell of damp dirt and earth was overwhelming as he fished the small keyring flashlight from his pocket.

Another scream echoed down the stairs and into the room he was navigating, before the gunshots and screaming expired. As Paul reached the edge of the room, near the false wall, he could hear nothing but rain drops hitting the floorboards above him.

Nineteen

*C*liff pulled up, stopping at the iron gate blocking their way from state-owned land to the private sanctuary of Granny Smith's Orchard.

"What do we do now?" Tyler asked from the back seat.

Cliff looked in the dash mirror and saw the two men sitting with guns across their laps. This was a bad idea, his gut kept saying, but he was determined to get it over with. "We get them to let us in, show them the warrant, sniff around a bit while the other three get some evidence, and then we call in the Feds. Done. Simple as that," he said, trying to sound confident. Judging by the look on Chuck's face, it hadn't worked.

He started to roll the window down to talk into the speaker when the gate buzzed and opened for them. Suddenly, Cliff felt like he'd been invited into the gates of hell, a nightmare about to begin.

"That was easy," Nick said, his voice thick from the back seat.

"A little too easy," chimed his partner Tyler.

"Keep quiet and follow my lead." Cliff threw the car in drive and followed the extended driveway up to the mansion at the end of it. The house was far too big for any normal people to live in, but he supposed the Smiths were anything but normal. He also thought they needed all the rooms to store their skeletons.

Rain still fell in heavy sheets from the sky, and it made Cliff wonder if it wasn't an omen from above. *Stay inside. Go home.* He shook his head to clear it and parked the car as close to the front porch as he could.

Inside the house, almost every light was off but the one at the front door. Inside, he thought he saw a shadow of a person on the right side of the home, but when he got out of the car and looked again, it was nothing but an empty window. *Quit jumping at shadows*, he thought, the last word making him shiver.

"Stay here," he said to the boys in the back seat. He nodded to Chuck, who got out of the passenger side, shutting the door a little too loudly.

Cliff hiked up the large wooden steps leading to the porch and was glad for the overhanging balcony that gave him reprieve from the downpour. He was getting too old to be walking around in the rain. As if on cue, his right knee flared up and he stumbled on the wooden slats; Chuck's arm was there to steady him.

Before he could ring the bell, the door creaked open to reveal a well put-together Katherine Smith. "Hello, Sheriff," she said, her voice bearing none of the venom from the other morning.

"Ma'am," he said, forcing himself to remember she probably wasn't an innocent in all of this mess. "We have a warrant to search the property, starting with this house."

He swore she almost smiled as she looked from him to Chuck, and past them to the two buffoons in the back seat.

"You really brought the cavalry, didn't you? Can I see this so-called warrant?" her voice purred out, and Cliff felt himself getting angry. The woman knew about the kids. She had to. She'd drugged Paul last night, and for all he knew, she was in on the whole thing.

"Don't get fresh with me, Katie." He said the

shortened version of her name, hoping it struck a chord, an old cop trick he hadn't pulled out in years.

"It's Katherine, and what are you looking for?" She grabbed the paper from his hand so quickly he felt the edge of it slice into his palm, leaving a clean cut.

"We have reason to believe Tommy O'Brian ended up on your property." He didn't want to say anything about Taylor, or any of the other countless victims. He couldn't show his hand too early on this bluff.

"You know that couldn't be," she said, but something changed in her face, and Cliff was going to poke it.

"Where's the old man? Where's Conway now?" he asked, throwing the sick patriarch's name at her.

Her mouth tightened in a straight line. "He's in bed. And for your information, I'm not sure he's going to make it through the night."

A series of flashes came down in the fields to the north, thunder booming heavily in the after effect.

"I'd like to speak with him." Cliff did, but what he really wanted was to keep the Smiths at the house, while the others went underneath.

More lightning, more thunder, then… something else. Cliff turned to the fields. That had been a revolver firing.

***

*D*arrel was pissed that Paul had decided to go his own way. Even in this situation, he went lone wolf. It figured.

The rain was soaking through his hat as they ran for the barn, Jason in a sling, the wound fresh on his shoulder and in their memory. Had it only been a couple days since they'd been there, sneaking into the structure like a bunch of fools? What was crazier was the fact they were going back.

They ran inside, and it was still unlocked, which surprised him. According to Cliff, they knew the guys had been there the other night. He looked around for any signs of an ambush but didn't see anyone. There were a lot of places to hide in here, though. The wall was lined with farming tools, and he shivered when he saw a rusty old scythe hanging there, like a bad omen. Hell, he'd probably seen too many scary movies.

The other night, he'd been so sure he'd seen a man in black; a shadow, perhaps, but he'd since convinced himself it was the adrenaline coursing through him that caused him to imagine something. How many times did people head to a strange basement on the job and see or hear something not there? All the time. Being in a hidden underground cellar, beneath a barn with a kid's bike, was probably about as good a place as any to let the fearful imagination run uninhibited.

"Looks clear to me," Jason said, his mini-camera strapped beside his headlamp. At least they were getting all of this on film.

Darrel nodded, his own camera and lamp jostled by the movement. "Let's go, buddy. This time, I swear I won't shoot you." He smiled at Jason, but the other man only grimaced, turning and heading for the hidden hatch. They'd done their best job of covering it up the other day, and it looked much the same as it had when they left it. Was it a little smoother now? Maybe Conway had tampered with it.

Jesus, he couldn't believe Beth's niece was gone. He hoped Beth was sitting in Chuck's with a damned rifle aimed at the door. If anything were ever to happen to Isabelle, Darrel was sure he'd go full berserker mode. Maybe he was beginning to understand Paul's actions a little more.

Darrel lifted the wooden door, letting it fall behind them, dust flying into the air. It clung to their wet clothes as they walked down the dirt steps.

Jason motioned Darrel ahead of him. Probably a good idea for the guy with two good arms to take the lead. Darrel knew this, but it didn't keep him from wishing he was back on his couch, watching the football game, or maybe sitting and talking with Beth. The whole experience made him wish he was a better man, a better husband. Paul's wife had left him high and dry, and as soon as he'd seen her, he was giving her attention and love. Darrel walked down the dirt tunnel, scared of what he might find at the other end. He told himself that if he made it out of here, he was going to be there for Beth and Isabelle.

"Let's check out the room," Jason whispered behind him. It was the same as they'd left it: blood splatter still there, a dark stain on the lighter packed-dirt floor.

Darrel led them out and down the hall, which narrowed as they went. Cobwebs crossed his path a few times, and he pictured monster spiders crawling on his jacket, heading for his ears. He was turned around now, not sure if he was heading toward the derelict house or away from it.

The path came to a fork: two options. Straight or right. "Shit," he said, not knowing which way to go.

"We could split up?" Jason said, lifting the last word to make it a question. They both knew that was a bad idea.

"No way, man." A noise came from the right. Scurrying. Squeaking. Three rats ran by them, heading straight down the tunnel. "Well, that didn't help. Go where the rats came from, or where they headed? Maybe something scared them toward us." Darrel was holding his shotgun, hands sweaty.

"Let's go right. Paul said they were intricate, but if he's

right, there should be a large room soon," Jason said.

It must be hard for the man, knowing Isaac was gone and probably down there somewhere, so close to Red Creek, but hidden away from everyone.

They moved on, the ceiling lower than before. It must have been a hundred yards or so when the entrance showed itself. To their left, there was an opening in the wall, half caved-in with dirt.

"This could be it," Jason said, his voice quivering and quiet.

Darrel stepped in front of him and started to dig dirt to the side, until there was enough space for them to get inside. His headlamp shone into the space, not finding a wall on the far end. It was deep.

He stepped inside, and the room was much cooler than the hallway. His flashlight shone across the room and he saw a line of bicycles, scooters, and skateboards. What the hell? His ankle rolled on what he thought was a rock, but when he looked down, he saw a white object. Kneeling, he turned it over, gasping at the small skull in his hand.

"I think we found it!" he exclaimed, trying to get into the hall again. He looked left and right frantically, but Jason was nowhere to be seen.

***

At first, the excitement of getting out of the room was enough to push the dread and fear from Paul's mind, but as he got farther from the hole in the wall, down the pitch-black tunnel, it crept back, ever so slowly, until he fell to the ground, crying silently.

He was just a boy. A thirteen-year-old boy. He'd only started getting hair in his pits, and Chrissy down the street was finally starting to notice him. But at that moment, he felt five, wanting his mommy to come and save him, to kiss his forehead and tell him everything was going to be okay. Instead, he had the feeling he was done, that he was going to die down here with dirt walls caving in around him, worms crawling through it and into his skin.

No! He wasn't going to lie down and die. Pushing aside the exhaustion and terror racking his body, he got up and kept moving. The pathways diverged in front of him. Should he go right or straight? He went right and was panting as he ran, sweat covering him, making his hair slap his eyes with each step.

His footsteps were muffled on the dirt floor but made a strange echo at one point. He stopped dead in his tracks at the noise. Feeling the wall, he found the opening. There was another room there. With great trepidation, he stepped into it, seeing a beam of light shine from above like a beacon from the heavens. Light meant outside! But the hole was at least ten feet above him, and tiny. It angled so the beam hit the floor near the far wall, and he let it lead him, his feet catching rocks or wood, almost sending him tripping a few times.

The light shone on a white object, and as Paul's eyes adjusted to the small amount of illumination, his brain finally processed what it was. It was a bone. It was like that time he'd spotted a spider in the forest floor, and as his peripheral vision caught up, he saw there were actually hundreds of them, crawling around, making for his legs. Only now, it was bones, skulls, and rib cages he was seeing everywhere. He screamed and headed for the door as a light came down the hallway, toward the room he was now trapped in.

Hoping it was someone who could help him, he called out to them.

"Help! Help me!" he called, whispering the word "mommy" in the incessant shrill yelling.

The light stopped, and a figure stepped into the room, lantern in his left hand, his shadow stretched out long to the right.

Paul couldn't make out the face in the dark, shadow-covered doorway. For a brief second, he thought help was there, but the man ignored his cries and turned, leaving Paul alone in the dark room, his eyes once again only seeing black.

Paul scrambled for the entrance, seeing the light bouncing up and down the way he'd come from. Wiping his wet face with a dirty sleeve, he ran the opposite way.

A few minutes later, he was at the end of the path, with nowhere to go. The wall was soft there too, and once again he dug, fingers still sore. He was sure he'd lost a couple of nails and was bleeding as he ripped through the dirt with a renewed fervor. That man was evil and needed to be stopped.

When the hole was enough for him to crawl through, he heard it. At first, he could hardly make out the sound over his own labored breathing, but it was there, coming toward him. He'd never heard a noise like it before. Close to a growl, but maybe pleasure too. A groan? He looked back but couldn't see anything. Maybe it was an animal? But it made no sound as the groaning closed in on him.

He wasn't going to wait around for it. He grunted and went head-first into the hole he'd dug, getting stuck at the waist. Dread coursed through him, thinking of some creature behind him, and not being able to do anything to stop it.

He stopped flailing his legs and started to dig around his waist with his hands. He was so tired, he almost considered stopping, letting it have him. But he didn't. He was nearly there, the dirt loosening, and he wiggled further, his legs pushing against the dirt floor on the other side. Right before he made it through, his legs became freezing cold, like they'd been dipped into ice water.

Soon he was scuttling away from the hole, once again finding himself in a room with no way out. Despair took over. He rolled on his side, too tired to do anything else. This room had light peering in from near the ceiling. Not a dirt room like the others. A part of him said that meant hope, but the majority stayed there, curled in a ball as it emerged from the hall he'd come from.

The light was dim, but it was enough for it to not be invisible to his eyes. No more blending into the darkness; the shadow blew in like a mist off the creek on an early spring morning. It stretched from the floor to the ceiling, pieces of misty shadow evaporating and replenishing as it moved.

Paul whimpered and froze in fear. The shadow man was here for him, just like it had been for all the rest of them, its lair full of their small undeveloped bones.

A noise came from outside the wall. Steps. Then a bang as someone hit the wall. The shadow reached for Paul's leg with a smoky tendril, but the wall behind him pried open. Paul stole a quick glance behind him, seeing a face staring at him, and when he turned back, the room was empty.

"You're okay, son. Everything is going to be okay." Then he was in the police officer's arms, but Paul felt far from safe. He knew it wasn't over. The shadow would be back for him. This he felt with every inch of his pained body.

Twenty

*P*aul pried open the false wall; apparently, it had been re-placed, if only with a half-assed attempt. The Smiths were obviously so over-confident in their community power that they never considered they'd be stopped. He'd seen a man down here that night, he now remembered that, and as soon as the memory was back, he knew it was Conway. The man had left him here to die like countless others, only Cliff had showed up, ruining that plan. Paul was really surprised he didn't get killed after that. Cold-blooded murder. But with the hypnosis, they assumed it was fine. Perhaps his mother had convinced her uncle to leave him alone. He was family, after all. But what did that mean for Paul's uncle who had been taken? Timothy was blood.

Had there ever been a shadow man? Adult Paul didn't believe so. It was Conway, and maybe his father before him, and so on. Was Katherine the newest generation of child killers? He hated that he shared bloodlines with the freaks, and they had his little girl now. It had to be Katherine. Conway was a sick old man. Wasn't he?

The wall Paul had climbed into still sat there, half-opened, and it only took him a handful of minutes to push the old dirt out of the way so he could slip into the tunnels. His body ached all over, but nothing was going to stop him. Deep down, a part of Paul was excited to be going back in there. He felt like it was his calling to end this family's psychotic killing spree. Taylor was bait, and that gave him confidence she wasn't going to be harmed. It was all he could do to keep from freaking out entirely, convince himself of that, over and over.

His flashlight was strapped to his belt in a makeshift holster, aiming straight ahead, but not giving a great beam. Inside the tunnel, he saw rats scurrying around, something he was glad to not have shared the tunnels with in the dark as a child. It had been terrifying enough. He did a three-sixty and saw the pathway went back toward the room full of bones he remembered, but also in the opposite direction. Either that hadn't been there before, or he hadn't known since it was pitch black back then. Paul was very thankful he had light this time.

The shotgun felt heavy in his hands as he crouched, walking down the hall toward the graveyard room. He suspected that was where he'd find Taylor, and as he took those last few steps, he hoped the two men were already there with her, protecting her from Conway.

When he entered the room, he saw a form by the wall.

"Taylor!" he called, but quickly saw it wasn't her.

"Paul, I'm sorry. She's not here," Darrel said, looking visibly shaken.

Shit. He'd been so sure this was the lair he was being led to.

"Where's Jason?" he asked.

The other man shrugged and nodded toward the entrance. "He disappeared. Like a minute ago. I have no idea where. I was doing a perimeter check, getting this all on film before getting the hell out of here. I think we have enough to nail the bastards, don't you?"

Paul wanted them nailed, all right, but he wanted his daughter back more. They had the leverage, and he needed to get it back. "Did you see any gas cans in the barn?"

Darrel looked at him silently for a moment before answering. "Yeah. I did. If they have any gas, we don't know how old it is, though."

"As long as it burns, I don't care."

***

*T*hey'd only heard a few gunshots ring out among the thunder, but Cliff had a sense of where it came from. His chest heaved as he ran in the rain, finding the little house he'd been at so many years ago. The rotted-out carcass of a home stood still, and he was surprised. He should have burned it to the ground along with the rest of the place, back when he'd had the chance.

His nerves were nearly shot as he walked into the doorway, gun raised in front of his chest. Chuck was behind him, and Cliff was glad for the backup. His gut was telling him something was wrong. Very wrong.

He got there expecting the old man to be sleeping, and the boys to radio in when they had the footage and proof. So far, radio silence. He was tempted to try them but was worried about giving their positions away if someone was stalking them. Damn it. Why did it have to be so complicated?

Chuck ran a flashlight around the room and stopped on two shapes piled on each other. Cliff knew a dead body when he saw one, and he was seeing two of them. Their familiar faces looked at him with dead eyes, their throats ripped open, blood everywhere.

Bile rose in his throat and he choked it back down. He'd have time for being sick later. Chuck, on the other hand, couldn't stop himself, and Cliff stepped to the side as he retched in the entranceway.

Cliff looked around for any sign of Paul or the others, but it was only these two here. A gun lay on the ground beside them. That explained the gunshots they'd heard.

"Back to the house. We need to speak to Conway now," Cliff said, Chuck nodding beside him. He'd left the two big guys back at the house to make sure Katherine didn't try to bolt. He hoped their combined brain power kept them from letting her talk her way out.

Back at the house, Cliff felt like he was a drowned rat, one in need of a warm dry bed and a scotch. Katherine was still flanked by the two men, and he smiled at that. Good boys.

"I need to see your grandfather. Now." Cliff stepped past her and into the house.

"Wait. He's not well! He needs to die in peace!" she called after him, but he'd had enough of Red Creek taking orders from Conway and his family. Cliff walked down the hall, looking back to see Tyler holding Katherine by the arms as she tried to fight her way through them. Her eyes were a rage, and their target was Cliff. He had to watch his back around that one.

He found a hallway past the huge living room, dying embers glowing softly in the massive fireplace. He checked the first room. It was a bathroom. The next room was locked, and before he tried his luck at kicking it open, he saw light flickering at the far end of the hall. The door was ajar.

His heart raced as he went into the room, his left foot stepping inside tentatively. Someone was in the bed, a lump under the blankets. Gotcha.

His radio beeped quietly, and Cliff cursed the timing. Conway hadn't moved yet.

"Come in," he said, pressing the talk button.

"We found it. The bones. They're in the tunnel. I have

it all on video." Darrel's voice was scratchy. Stressed.

"Good job, boys. Is everyone okay?" he asked.

"Jason's missing. No sign of Taylor. Do you have Conway?" This time, it was Paul's voice on the other side.

"I'm in his room. I'm about to rouse him. He might be sleeping."

"Be careful. If you smell smoke, get out of there."

Cliff was about to question that, but he left Paul to it. He wasn't sure what the man was going to burn in the late autumn rainstorm of a century. It was as wet as the Atlantic out there.

He moved to the bedside, looking for signs of breathing. Katherine had said the old man was near death. Maybe he'd finally given up the ghost.

"Conway?" he said. With the hand not holding the revolver, he reached for the white linens and pulled them down slowly.

A middle-aged woman lay there, blood pooling under her cold body.

Cliff jumped back, startled by the corpse, and tripped, falling to the ground. A shadow emerged from the wall and moved toward him.

***

*T*hey were back at the tunnel under the old house. Paul had started thinking of them as the catacombs, the longer he spent down here. He saw bones stuck into the walls and ceiling; Darrel was white as a ghost and shaking by the time they were back at the far side of the passages. A long line of gunky gasoline and kerosene snaked its way from the barn to their current spot.

"You sure this is a good idea?" Darrel asked.

Paul wasn't. "Yeah. Go back to the barn and watch your back. This way has to lead to the big house. It's the only place we haven't been yet."

"Then let me come with you. You can't do this alone."

"Try to find Jason while you're at it. And get the camera back topside to Cliff." Paul hoped like hell his little girl was at the end of the black tunnel, and he hated telling Darrel to go in the other direction. "They're going to need that if things go south down here." He looked to the stream of liquid soaking into the floor as they spoke.

"Don't let anything happen to you. Beth will kill me." Darrel tried to give him a smile, but it was more of a grimace. Paul was starting to like the guy.

He clapped his brother-in-law on the arm and watched him run back the way they'd come from. Taylor. He had to find her. It had been almost an hour since she'd been taken.

The tunnel leading from the old dead house to the mansion was a little taller and wider. Maybe Conway used it more. It would make sense. Paul traveled for a few hundred yards, shotgun barrel resting on his left forearm and pointing forward, gasoline still being dripped along the floor with his left hand.

Stopping, he heard noise from ahead. Was that music? He strained his ears and could make out the melancholic sounds of a violin bouncing off the dirt walls toward him. Sweat beaded down his face, and he tried to wipe it with his right shoulder. It stung his eyes as he neared the source of the music. The hall bent, angling slightly to the right. Eventually, it straightened out and he saw light.

The end of the hall.

No more rooms to the sides. No more pathway underground. Just the space at the end of the hall, a room with lighting. He tried to think of the distance and guessed it was likely he stood directly under the mansion now. He let the large gas canister settle to the ground.

"Come in, Paul," a voice said. He peered into the room, the lanterns overbearing after being in the near dark for the last hour. He held the shotgun up, not willing to set foot inside until he saw what he was up against.

A muffled voice cried out, and he got the lay of the land on his second peek inside, his eyes finally better acclimated to the light. Taylor was inside, hands behind her back, duct tape over her mouth. She was squirming, and fear swam deep in her bright wet eyes.

"Taylor! Daddy's here. Don't worry. I'll protect you," he called from the hall, his back tight against the wall so he was hidden.

He could hear her muffled cries get louder at his voice. At least he'd found her. Stealing one more glance, he saw the man who had spoken to him. He sat in a chair, knife in hand, with a three-piece suit on.

It was Conway, and Paul felt his stomach tighten at the look in the old man's face. It was a man on his deathbed.

He didn't see anyone else inside, so he stepped in, moving the shotgun to either side of the room to make sure it was clear. It was just the three of them, Vivaldi coming from an old record player's speakers on the far side of the room, stairs leading upwards past them.

The floor was still dirt, but a large decorative carpet lay in the center, like adding décor spruced up the monster's space. Humanizing Conway wasn't something Paul was willing to do.

"You're a bastard, Conway," Paul said before thinking. He needed to be tactful, especially since the madman had a knife to his little princess.

This only made Conway's eyes glitter, and he sat up a little straighter. Paul remembered having a dog when he was only a little boy. It had been his father's dog even before he married, and Paul knew the look of an animal who knew it was about to die. That pooch's eyes were wet and resigned as little Paul had petted him, telling him it was going to be okay. Conway had that look now, and Paul was more than happy to do him a favor and speed it up.

"Paul, my boy, you don't know the half of it." His voice was soft, hoarse, wet. He started to cough, and Paul looked at his daughter's eyes, locking in and squinting ever so slightly, something he used to do to her across a room, that she called "sparkle eyes." She visibly calmed down ever so slightly, so he did it again, while Conway held the knife shakily during his fit.

"As you can see, I don't have a lot of time. What do you know about the Smiths, son?" Conway asked once there was enough air in his tired lungs to speak.

"I know you're a bunch of murderous assholes. Killing children gets you guys off, has for a few generations, hasn't it? How did it work? Your grandpa taught your dad, then he taught you as well? Did they touch you too, Conway? Did they tell you to keep that a secret as well as the killing?" Paul didn't know where this was coming from, but he was pissed off. The bones of dead children lay in the dirt all around the underground of the orchard, and this smug prick was the reason.

Conway slowly shook his head, making a *tsk*ing sound with his mouth. "You have it all wrong, son. Have you forgotten that you're one of us?"

Paul aimed the gun at the old man then. "I never have been, and never will be, one of you."

A wet laugh came from the man's mouth as the song hit its crescendo. The record skipped and started to loop a few notes over and over, distracting Paul in the process.

"You really don't remember, do you? That doctor was worth every penny."

"Oh, I remember all right. I remember you down there that day. I remember you grabbing my leg as Cliff rescued me. Give me my girl, and I'll let you die in peace in your horror hotel down here." Paul lowered the gun.

"You're correct. I was down there, but it wasn't me who took you now, was it? I was weak, letting it get one of our own like that. It paid dearly for that mistake, but we kept going. No harm, no foul. The deal was broken once before."

"Timothy," Paul found himself whispering.

"Yes, Timothy. Only that time, we offered him to seal the deal. It was getting too wild; we needed it to know we meant business."

The man was losing it. What the hell was he talking about? Conway didn't actually expect him to believe his own urban legend, did he?

"Either way, we'll renew our pact once again, or my dear Katherine will continue the legacy. We only need another sacrifice in the creek first, don't we? Another child of the blood will do just fine," Conway said, his right hand grabbing Taylor, and his left lifting a knife toward her.

A gunshot rang from behind Conway, and Paul saw a red blotch open on the old man's forehead. It spread out, blood spilling in droves down his face. He slumped forward, taking Taylor down with him. With her hands behind her back, she couldn't stop from landing on her face.

Paul was there in an instant, rolling her over and cutting the twine behind her back with his box cutter. Cliff was slumped on the ground, blood staining his uniform at his chest and stomach.

There was a look of abject terror on his face. He was dying.

Paul held Taylor in his arms and looked where the slouching sheriff was pointing.

Up the wooden stairs.

At first, Paul saw nothing; then it passed over Cliff, a long finger extending out, smoky blackness wisping out as it sliced Cliff's throat. The shadow man was real, and it had ended the one man who'd cared enough to save him once, and now twice. Pushing the emotions and dread coursing through his veins aside, Paul backed up to the door.

Its head was a faceless circle, red eyes glowing ever-so-slightly as they turned to the body on the carpet. It shrieked as it saw Conway lying there dead, as horrible a noise as Paul had ever heard.

How was he supposed to stop a shadow?

It was easily ten feet tall, and as it got closer, the black-ness seemed to solidify, reaching a deadly arm for the two of them.

Paul slung Taylor over his right shoulder and fired the shotgun at the monster. It squealed as the shells hit it, air showing between its abdomen and chest. The smoke cleared and filled in again. Now it looked angry as it flew for them.

He dropped the gun and ran. His legs pumped like they hadn't in years. Years of running in the park took over, and he raced through the corridor like a bat out of hell, his pre-cious cargo a dead weight against his back.

Paul's radio beeped, and he heard Darrel's voice over the tiny speaker. Jason was still down there. He wouldn't leave. He was coming for Paul.

He heard all this as he spotted his friend running for him. The smell of gasoline was overwhelming now. They must have doused the whole place. Shrieks followed after him, the thing still giving chase.

Paul peeked back, seeing the demon racing right be-hind him. When he looked back, he saw the gas can too late.

The floor came at him in a rush as he fell, Taylor springing off his shoulder. He could hear the shadow man still shrieking loudly. Angrily.

Paul forced himself to get up, and Taylor was already on her feet. Wobbly, but on her feet.

"Jason, we need to get the hell out of here! It's real. Cliff's dead. Conway's dead. The shadow is coming now!" he yelled at the man, but Jason just gave him a stony smile.

"Paul, go. Get to the barn and drop a match," Jason said, the sounds getting closer by the second.

"But, Jason…" Paul was being shoved in the back by his old best friend, and soon he was running, knowing there was no way he could help his lost buddy.

***

"*Y*ou killed my boy, you sick son of a bitch!" Jason yelled at the approaching monster. As the thing neared him, he could only think about saving his old friend and his daughter, and of his own son. Jason held his gun in the air and pointed it at the creature, his finger twitching on the trigger over and over. The shots didn't even slow it, black ichor spraying behind it as it floated toward him.

He turned quickly and saw that Paul was well on his way. He would make it out. Jason only hoped that burning the mother down would kill this demon once and for all.

The shadow was close now, and Jason stood firmly, closing his eyes momentarily. He pictured Isaac being born. He'd never been prouder of anything in his life. Mary lying in the hospital bed, face drenched in sweat, their baby boy swaddled and in her arms. He saw Isaac at his first birthday party, then on his first day of school. He saw him as they played catch in the field, trying to get Isaac good enough to make the Little League starting pitching role. Tears streamed from Jason's eyes as the shadow approached him, hands extended toward his throat.

***

*P*aul kept moving, feeling Taylor coming around. The smell of gas was so strong, he felt light-headed by the time he found the room he'd originally woke up in when he was thirteen.

"Daddy," she said, jostling around in his arms. He'd had to pick her up again, and his body was protesting the extra weight, making him feel like he was close to passing out.

"Get up the stairs!" he yelled, and she obliged, her little legs going faster than he'd ever seen them move.

He followed closely and slid the matches from the diner out of his pocket. With a flick of his wrist, he tossed the flame. It landed, and when he thought he had to throw another, it caught, the line of gas suddenly dancing in red-hot flames. Inside the barn, he could still hear thunder, rain pounding down on the old wooden roof, and he picked Taylor up, walking away from the trap door, which he kicked shut.

"You're here. Where's Jason?" Darrel asked, thick with worry.

Paul shook his head and walked away, holding his daughter close.

Sirens rang in the distance, the smell of smoke starting to make its way above ground.

Taylor was crying into his shoulder as he walked outside, the rain still not letting up.

"It's okay, honey. It's okay." Paul said the words as much for himself as he did for her.

Twenty-One

"*T*hanks for sticking around. It means a lot to us," Beth said, squeezing Paul's hand.

He looked into the back of the full truck and pulled the sliding door down, flipping the latch closed.

Their old home was finally empty, the For Sale sign stuck into place on the front yard. Taylor was playing with Isabelle, Terri watching every movement closely. They didn't know if the thing was dead, but Paul imagined it was linked to that spot one way or another, or to Conway. All he knew was he would be leaving in the morning and getting the hell away from Red Creek once again.

"You thinking of moving?" he asked his sister, hoping she was going to say yes. Over the past few days, he'd been trying to sell her on the idea, but even with all that had gone down, she seemed reluctant.

"Mom's still here. My home is here."

"There are a lot of places for Mom in New York, you know." He knew it wasn't going to work, but he had Beth in his life now, and he wasn't ready to let that go.

She shook her head. "There's nothing in that big city for us. We're simple folks." Beth smiled, watching Darrel play dolls with the girls on the front sidewalk.

Paul looked past him and toward the old pathway at the end of the block. Its power over him seemed to be gone for good. No more blackouts, no more bleeding nose, no more anything. It was only a pathway now, again. To him, that was a huge sign the monster might be dead.

"How about some pizza?" Paul called to the group. The girls cheered, and Terri smiled back at him. God, he loved that woman. He was so glad to have her back in his life.

Taylor plopped into the back seat, and Isabelle joined her. Apparently, the two of them were joined at the hip now. When they were on the road, Terri reached over and laid her hand on his.

"You still have the paperwork to look at, you know," she said, nodding to the file folder sitting on his front dash. "You told Don you'd have an answer by today."

"It's not up to me. It's up to us," he said, happy at how quickly he was willing to let her off with leaving him and taking Taylor. He knew he wasn't the easiest guy to live with, and his life now made more sense than it ever had before. He was so glad they were back in his now.

"Then I say we stay there. Keep the condo."

"Yay! I hate LA!" Taylor said from the back seat.

Paul stuck his hand between the two front seats and grabbed her leg playfully. "Hey, no eavesdropping!"

"I love you, Daddy," she said. This time, the fun was gone from her voice. She had been through so much, he couldn't believe how well she was taking it all.

"I love you too, honey bear."

***

"*I*s Santa still coming?" Taylor asked, staring out the large window that overlooked Central Park. Snow was coming down in sheets, and the city was becoming a winter wonderland.

"Of course he is. Santa lives for snow." Terri poured a glass of wine and passed it to Paul.

He was so glad to be home. The craziness of Red Creek felt like it was years ago, not months. The transition for Terri and Taylor was seamless, Taylor reconnecting with old friends, the happy couple reuniting with theirs. Most of them even pretended not to be upset with Terri about leaving. Paul really couldn't have asked for more.

The smell of roasting ham emanated from the kitchen, and he couldn't help but realize how much better his home was with actual life and love in it.

"Are you almost done for the day?" Terri asked him, motioning to his laptop. He was wrapping up his book, the one he'd started before Red Creek took over. It was a great book, and he smelled another bestseller after all these years. His agent thought so too.

"I can be," he said. His laptop started to ring, showing a video call coming in.

Paul accepted, and his sister's face appeared, looking younger and healthier than two months ago. Paul thought they all did.

"Hey, sis," he said. Taylor ran over, saying hi to her aunt before heading back to the living room to watch the Grinch again.

"Hi, Paul. Is Taylor gone?" she asked quietly, her face cut in a serious look.

He nodded. "She's watching TV. What's up?"

"We heard that Katherine Smith was found dead in her room at the Max. It was ruled a suicide."

Sweat dripped down Paul's armpits as he took in the news, his body suddenly flushed. Why should he care? She was a horrible woman who'd admitted to knowing everything. She claimed to know nothing about a shadow or monster, but blamed Conway for it. She was still given ten years. But suicide? She was related to Paul by blood, and he felt a little sadness that it had to end like that.

"How about the orchard? They keeping it fenced off?" he asked.

"Yeah. They say they need to do more tests, but I think the new sheriff is more than happy to keep the red tape up as long as he can. Especially since half the old earth under the orchard caved in after the fire."

Paul laughed. "And how is Sheriff Tyler doing?" He pictured the big man wearing the badge and couldn't help but feel proud of the guy.

"He's doing great. For the first time, it feels like the cloud is lifted from Red Creek. Maybe the town can build on the momentum and become something." Beth was thinking of running for the Chamber of Commerce, and Paul had urged her to go through with it. To his surprise, so had Darrel. According to his sister, the man was way more attentive and caring than he'd ever been.

"You guys are still coming down for Christmas, right?" Paul asked, really looking forward to having them over. It was all Taylor could talk about all week, and that was with seeing presents under the tree. "I know it's not easy, but could you bring mom with you?" Paul felt a new connection to his estranged mother. He finally understood her motives, and wished he had more time with her over the last twenty years.

"You bet your life on it. Love you, big brother," Beth said.

"Love you, little sis," Paul replied, shutting the call down.

Terri called from the kitchen that dinner would be ready in five minutes.

Paul closed his computer and carried it under his arm, heading for his office. Plugging it in to charge, he let his gaze linger on the snow falling. Was there anything better than Central Park at Christmas time? He loved the city and was so happy they'd decided to stay.

Something caught the corner of his peripheral vision out there. A black shape moved smoothly, passing under the street lanterns in the park, snow dancing at the movement.

He closed his eyes, and when he opened them again, there was nothing. Doctor Norman had told him this was possible, for his subconscious to project things that weren't real. Maybe that was what happened under the orchard, he'd said. Paul was hesitant to admit, two months later, that he thought the good doctor might be right.

One last glance, and there was nothing but soft snow falling in the distance.

"Paul, dinner's on," Terri called from the other room.

Yes. He was glad to have his family back.

END

About the Author

Nathan Hystad is an author from Sherwood Park, Alberta, Canada. When he isn't writing novels, he's running a small publishing company, Woodbridge Press.

Keep up to date with his new releases by signing up for his newsletter at www.nathanhystad.com

30496461R00144

Made in the USA
San Bernardino, CA
26 March 2019